Harper heard the old Chevy roar into the driveway and rushed to the window. There he was. Lean. Tan. Shirtless. His golden hair bronzed by the sun, his hundred-watt smile piercing through his obvious exhaustion. . . .

She opened the window, about to call out, to wave—then thought better of it and just watched. He was her oldest friend, the boy who knew all of her secrets and liked her anyway—the boy she'd recently discovered was a man she wanted to be with. Might even be in love with.

There was just one problem with the picture-perfect romance—the picture-perfect girlfriend. Beautiful Beth. Blond Beth. Bland and boring Beth.

Lately, the Blond One was all Adam could talk about, and it was driving Harper slowly but surely insane.

Harper slammed the window shut and crossed the room to her bed, which was covered in clothes—a haphazard pile of unsuitable first-day-of-school possibilities. . . .

She needed something special, something that would make her look good. *Really* good, Harper mused, fingering a lime green miniskirt that she knew would show off her tan—and potentially, depending on how far she bent over, a lot more.

It was simple. Harper wanted Adam—and Harper always got what she wanted.

It was just a matter of figuring out how.

SEVEN DEADLY SINS

Lust

Soon to be committed:
Envy

SEVEN DEADLY SINS

ROBIN WASSERMAN

SIMON PULSE
New York   London   Toronto   Sydney

〰SIMON PULSE
An imprint of Simon & Schuster
Children's Publishing Division
1230 Avenue of the Americas, New York, NY 10020
Copyright © 2005 by Robin Wasserman
All rights reserved, including the right of reproduction in whole or in part in any form.
SIMON PULSE and colophon are registered trademarks of Simon & Schuster, Inc.
Designed by Ann Zeak
The text of this book was set in Bembo.
Manufactured in the United States of America
First Simon Pulse edition October 2005
10 9 8 7 6 5 4 3 2 1
Library of Congress Control Number 2005920706
ISBN-13: 978-0-689-87782-7
ISBN-10: 0-689-87782-X

For Susie

This momentary joy breeds months of pain;
This hot desire converts to cold disdain.
—William Shakespeare, "The Rape of Lucrece"

Don't put me off, 'cause I'm on fire,
And I can't quench my desire.
Don't you know that I'm burning up for your love,
You're not convinced that that is enough.
—Madonna, "Burning Up"

chapter

1

"And it was the best sex I'd ever had." Harper finished off the story with her favorite line and a lascivious grin.

The other girls tanning themselves on the makeshift beach (though chaise lounges plus backyard plus desert sun and margaritas did not an island paradise make) sighed appreciatively. All but Miranda, who rolled her eyes and—just barely—stifled a snort. Harper had already given her best friend the full download on this guy, so she knew very well that the previous evening's encounter had been nothing if not nasty, brutish, and (perhaps mercifully) short.

But Harper knew Miranda would keep her mouth shut. After all, when had she ever dared ruin a Harper Grace story? Never—which is exactly why their friendship had lasted so long.

"So what now?" Beth asked, tucking her long blond hair behind her ears. A nervous habit. Miranda and Harper exchanged a smirk: The hallmark of any good Beth Manning imitation was to get the hair tuck just right, at a frequency of about one per every three sentences. "Are you going to see him again?"

Harper just laughed and shook her head, a crest of wavy auburn hair whipping across her face. "Maybe when hell freezes over—or when pashminas come back in style—but not before. Not even great sex is worth dealing with *that* again, if you know what I mean. . . ."

The girls all burst into laughter and, clinking their plastic margarita glasses, toasted—to good stories, and better decisions. In the rock-paper-scissors of life in Grace, California, sex sometimes trumped boredom—but often (given the quality of guys available in Grace) it was the other way around.

But this—sun, fun, and booze, girls only—this was the life. They'd been meeting once a week all summer, setting up shop in Harper's backyard—and given that the rest of the week was generally filled with sweat, lethargy, and dead-end part-time jobs off the highway, serving fast food or gas or porn to skeezy travelers, "beach day" was always a highlight. Even if instead of sexy bronzed lifeguards, they were watched over by a couple of spiny, brownish cacti. Even if the only available view consisted of the low-slung hills that loomed on the fringes of town, lumps of dirt and dust irregularly spotted with scrub brush as if they'd been struck by a fatal dose of desert leprosy. Even if the only water in sight sat warming in the pitcher Harper periodically tipped into the mouth of the tequila bottle, replacing what she'd taken in hopes her parents would remain none the wiser. So what? The sun still bore down on them from a cloudless sky, mixing with their carefully applied sunscreen to create the picture-perfect tan. The day was hot, the drinks were cool, and it was still summer. At least for now.

"But the really unbelievable thing——," Harper began again, then stopped abruptly. "Aren't you a little old for the Peeping Tom act?" she called out in a louder voice, gesturing toward the sliding glass door of the house next door, where a strikingly handsome face had just shown itself. Harper's neighbor, and another highlight of the week: the handsome, hunky, and utterly unavailable Adam Morgan. It wouldn't be a day at the beach without putting in some scoping time. And there was no one better to scope—too bad he always showed up fully clothed.

Adam crept into the backyard with one hand splayed loosely over his eyes.

"Is it safe for me to look, or have you ladies started up the nude tanning portion of your afternoon?" he asked, as the girls frantically threw themselves into poses that maximized their good parts—not that, in their skimpy bikinis, there was much of anywhere to hide the bad.

"This is reality, Adam, not your favorite porn movie," Harper drawled. "What are you doing here, anyway? Shouldn't you be off somewhere celebrating your last day of freedom? There's only"—she checked her watch—"nineteen hours left before that first bell rings."

"Yeah, good-bye summer, hello torture. Don't worry, I'm headed out to the courts now—just thought I'd stop by to say hello." He ruffled Harper's hair and then squeezed onto the plastic chaise lounge next to Beth, slinging a tan, well-muscled arm around his girlfriend.

"Nice to see you, too," Beth giggled. "Now get out of here so that Harper can finish telling us about her date."

"Another date?" He flashed Harper a knowing grin and took a swig from Beth's drink. "I just hope you're not teaching my girl here any of your tricks." He winked at Harper, then leaned over to give Beth a quick peck on the lips.

That was Adam—equal opportunity friend, one-woman man.

Beth nuzzled against her boyfriend. "Don't worry, Adam—I think Harper's got all the guys in town staked out as her own personal property. I guess I'm just stuck with you."

No one who wasn't watching for it would have noticed, but with those words, Harper's face turned a definite shade of pale. And who could blame her? Listening to the happy couple's flirtatious simpering was enough to turn anyone's stomach. And given that Beth had only been invited in the first place by virtue of her connection to Adam, it seemed more than a bit inappropriate for her to be teasing Harper about her conquests. It was one thing when Harper and Miranda laughed about all the men— but coming out of Beth's mouth, it just made Harper sound like . . . well . . . a slut.

But Harper suppressed the nasty comeback that threatened to leap off her tongue. No reason to let the blah blonde spoil her perfectly pleasant afternoon. Besides, Beth would learn her lesson—soon enough.

"I mean, come on, Harper," Beth continued, oblivious to the dangerous ground she was treading. "After all these years and all these dates, is there even anyone left? Or have you been through every eligible guy in town?"

Harper aimed her most sugary grin at the happy couple,

her gaze lingering on Adam's handsomely chiseled face and brawny shoulders.

"Not yet, Beth," she said, slowly shaking her head. "Trust me—not yet."

With a sneer, Kaia wearily waved away the stewardess—or flight attendant, if you wanted to bother being PC about it. Which she didn't, of course. Who cared if she offended little blond Charlotte, washed-up beauty queen from Tennessee, or Ricky, her so-gay-here-come-the-stereotype-police-to-come-drag-him-away partner in crime? As if she wanted a rancid plate of underdone potatoes and gravy-swaddled mystery meat sitting in front of her for the rest of the flight. She didn't need airplane food to make her nauseous—these days, life was doing a good enough job of that on its own.

She squirmed in her seat, trying her best not to touch the greasy arm of the woman next to her, who'd only barely managed to squeeze her rolls of fat into the narrow seat. Talk about airplane clichés—now all she needed was the screaming baby.

THUD.

Oh, that's right—the universe's central casting office had instead saddled her with a bratty five-year-old who had a bad case of ADD and, apparently, a spastic kicking problem.

"Now, now, Taylor," a weary voice behind her said. "We don't kick the seat in front of us—it's not nice."

Kaia wanted to turn around and explain to little Taylor and his wimpy mother exactly what would happen to "us" if the kicking continued throughout the rest of this interminable flight—but she thought better of it.

Simple math: The in-flight movie (some tedious Adam Sandler bomb) would only last two hours, the flight would last at least six—she needed to save *some* entertainment options for later.

THUD.

Kaia sighed, pulled out her iPod, and tried to relax. As the Shins warbled in her ear, she practiced the breathing exercises that Rashi—her mother's yoga instructor, life coach, and all-around personal guru—had taught her last year. Breathe in, breathe out. Clear your mind. Go to your safe place.

Of course it was all bullshit—ancient wisdom dished out at $300 an hour, maybe—but bullshit nonetheless.

She just needed to stop dwelling. *Stress causes wrinkles,* Kaia reminded herself, and just because her mother was the reigning Botox queen of Manhattan didn't mean that she was eager to claim the throne anytime soon. She needed to calm down . . . but exactly how was she supposed to do that with her hideous new life rushing toward her at six hundred miles an hour?

It was bad enough that she was being shipped across the country like a piece of furniture. (Last summer, for example, her mother had decided that her grandmother's mahogany armoire clashed with the new Danish modern decor and shipped it out to her father. This summer's "out of sight, out of mind" shipment was Kaia.) Bad enough that she was going to miss this year's Central Park fall gala, the winter benefit season, *all* the La Perla sample sales—basically, every social event of the year. And she was sure that her so-called friends would waste no time in making her so-called boyfriend (okay, *all* her boyfriends) feel a little less lonely.

It was certainly bad enough that she was going to be stuck in the middle of nowhere—literally exiled to the desert, and for a lot longer than forty days and forty nights. That tomorrow she'd be facing her first day at some hick school sure to be filled with a bunch of losers destined for community college or *ranching* school, and who probably thought that Gucci was a neato name for a pet cow.

THUD.

She winced. (One more time and that kid was going to learn about the emergency exits the hard way.)

It was bad enough, to sum up, that the plane was hurtling toward a father she barely knew, a town whose name she couldn't remember, a year in hicksville hell—

THUD.

All that was bad enough—but honestly, did they really have to make her fly *coach*?

Kane Geary released the ball from his fingertips and then turned away, as if to demonstrate his lack of interest in following its perfect arc across the court. But he grinned as, a moment later, he heard the swish.

"Check it out," he bragged. "Nothing but net."

Adam grabbed the ball and tossed it back to his friend in disgust. He should have known his early lead was just a false hope. He'd known Kane for almost ten years—and the last time Kane lost a game of pickup ball, they'd both been about three feet tall. Kane may have been too lazy to show up for practices (so lazy, in fact, that he'd been thrown off the Haven High team in ninth grade, never to return), but when it came to actual games, he hated to lose. And thus, never did.

In other words, trailing by seven points and about five

minutes away from utter exhaustion, Adam had no chance whatsoever.

"Okay, Shaq, how about we wrap it up for today?" he suggested. The tiny basketball court behind the high school offered no opportunities for shade (much like the rest of town), their bottles of water were long since empty, and after an hour of running back and forth in the searing desert heat, Adam's shorts looked like he'd just worn them in the shower. His shirt, now balled up at the foot of the basket, had long since become a lost cause, and his sweaty chest glistened in the sun.

Kane, on the other hand, looked as if he'd just stepped out of his air-conditioned Camaro; only a small trickle of sweat tracing a path down his cheekbone betrayed the afternoon's exertion in 103-degree heat.

Kane tossed up a casual layup, which rolled once around the rim and then tipped away, on the wrong side of the net. *At least the guy misses sometimes,* Adam told himself. Small comfort.

"In awe of my superior skills?" Kane smirked, jogging down the court to grab the rebound. "Terrified of going head-to-head against the reigning champ? Worried that by the time the winter season starts, you'll be so demoralized that you'll have to drop off your little team?"

Adam laughed, imagining the look on his coach's face after hearing that his star forward was too *sad* to play that season. Yeah, coach would just love that.

Adam darted across the court and snatched the ball away from Kane, shooting a jump shot from mid-court and watching with satisfaction as the ball soared toward the net.

Three points. Sweet.

"More like I need to get home and make myself pretty for my girlfriend," he corrected Kane. "I hope all those dreams of basketball glory keep you warm tonight while you're sitting home *alone* eating leftovers and watching *The Simpsons*. Beth and I will be thinking of you—oh, wait, no we won't."

"Very funny. You should take that act on the road." Kane shook his head in disbelief. "I still don't understand what the hottest girl in school sees in a loser like you—you're just lucky I'm too busy to give you much competition." Kane palmed the ball and tossed Adam his shirt, and they took off for the parking lot. In the waning hours of summer vacation it was still empty, Kane's lovingly restored Camaro and Adam's rusted Chevy the only evidence of human life in the concrete wasteland. As they walked, both guys tried their best to avoid looking directly at the low-slung red building that would soon imprison them for the next nine months. Ignoring the inevitable may have been a feeble defense, but it was all they had.

"And by 'busy,' I assume you mean hopping in and out of bed with half the cheerleading squad and three fifths of the girl's field hockey team?" Adam retorted. With his close-cropped black hair, piercing brown eyes, and impeccable physique, Kane could have any girl he wanted. And Adam knew that by now, he'd pretty much had them all.

"Dude, you know what they say—idle hands are the devil's plaything." Kane gave Adam his best Sunday school smile. "You gotta keep them busy doing *something*."

"You're disgusting, you know that?" Adam slapped his friend good-naturedly on the back. "You give us all a bad name."

Kane shoved him in return, then began idly dribbling the ball as they walked.

"Seriously, Adam, I know she's hot, but you've been with her awhile—aren't you bored yet? There's bound to be some freshman cuties this year. . . ."

Adam bristled and walked a step faster, wondering—not for the first time—how disgusted Beth would be if she knew the kind of guy his best friend really was. Sure, she'd seen plenty of Kane and was already distinctly unimpressed—but that was Kane in good behavior mode. Kane: Uncensored was not a pretty sight.

"I mean, she's gorgeous and all," Kane continued, "but she seems a little uptight, if you know what I mean."

Adam whirled on him, eyes blazing with anger.

"Enough! Don't talk about her like that. She's not one of your brainless floozies. She's—" Adam cut himself off. He wasn't about to explain to Kane how Beth was different from all the girls he'd dated before (especially since he still didn't really understand it himself). Wasn't going to tell him about how beautiful she looked in the desert moonlight or how he could tell her things, secrets, about himself and his life and his dreams that he'd never told anyone before. He certainly wasn't telling Kane that he thought he might be in love with her.

They were guys, after all, and friendship—even best friendship—had its limits.

"Whatever," he finally continued. "Just give it a rest, okay? Beth and I are *not* breaking up anytime soon."

Kane winked and gave Adam an intentionally hokey leer.

"No problem. I guess if I had a girl like that willing to

climb into bed with me, I wouldn't want to let her out anytime soon either."

Adam flushed and said a silent prayer to whoever watched over sex-obsessed teenagers that Kane wouldn't notice his sudden silence and obvious discomfort. Beth was willing to climb into the bed, all right. She would lie there next to him, her perfect body nestled against his. She would kiss him, and caress him, and drive him crazy with desire, and—

And that was about it.

Harper heard the old Chevy roar into the driveway and rushed to the window. There he was. Lean. Tan. Shirtless. His golden hair bronzed by the sun, his hundred-watt smile piercing through his obvious exhaustion.

Adam. Her next-door neighbor. Her childhood friend—her partner for swimming lessons, playground dates, imaginary tea parties, and the occasional game of doctor.

And now, years later: Homecoming king. Star of the swim team. The basketball team. The lacrosse team. Basically, an All-American high school stud. None of which meant much to her, considering how lame their school was, and the fact that she usually saw sports as a crutch for the mentally weak. Besides, that's not what she saw when she looked at him. Or, at least, not all she saw, not anymore.

She opened the window, about to call out to him, to wave—then thought better of it and just watched. What she saw when she looked at him was her oldest friend, the boy who knew all of her secrets and liked her anyway—

the boy she'd recently discovered was a man she wanted to be with. Might even be in love with.

What a hassle.

The poor little overlooked best friend, languishing in the shadows, the man of her dreams blinded by the bright glare of puppy love. Tossing his true soul mate aside in favor of a human Barbie doll. It was such a pathetic cliché—and Harper didn't do clichés. She liked to consider herself unique, and she wasn't a huge fan of seeing her life turn into a second-rate knockoff of a third-rate teen chick flick. Especially one that starred her as the weepy protagonist too wimpy to open her mouth and take what she wanted.

But on the other hand—just look at him.

Postgame, Adam was hot, sweaty, and shirtless, and his taut body gleamed in the sun. Harper couldn't take her eyes off him—that tan six-pack, those firm pecs, the broad biceps that, if she used her imagination, she could feel ever so gently tightening around her. . . .

There was just one problem with the picture-perfect romance—the picture-perfect girlfriend. Beautiful Beth. Blond Beth. Bland and boring Beth.

Lately, the Blond One was all Adam could talk about, and it was driving Harper slowly but surely insane. He was probably even now heading inside to call her, to whisper sweet nothings in his lilting Southern accent (an adorable holdover from an early childhood in South Carolina). He was probably already planning some sickeningly sweet, romantic candlelit dinner for their last night of summer. He was just that kind of guy. It was disgusting. And it should have been her.

Harper slammed the window shut and crossed the

room to her bed, which was covered in clothes—a haphazard pile of unsuitable first-day-of-school possibilities. She burrowed through them in frustration, wondering how it was possible that with all these clothes, she never had anything to wear.

The beaded yellow tank top with pleated ruffles and an off-center sash that had looked so promising in the store? Hideous.

The stonewashed denim jacket that hugged her curves and made her feel like a supermodel? *So* last season.

The tan blouse and matching scarf her mother had brought home as a surprise last month? Yeah, maybe—if she was *forty*. And was a desperate housewife.

No. She needed something special, something that would make her look good. *Really* good, Harper mused, fingering a lime green miniskirt that she knew would show off her tan—and potentially, depending on how far she bent over, a lot more.

It was simple. Harper wanted Adam—and Harper always got what she wanted.

It was just a matter of figuring out how.

chapter

2

Senior year, day one.

Harper sighed. An hour into the year, and it already felt like an eternity. At least she'd already managed to snag a coveted Get-Out-of-Class-Free pass, this time in the guise of eagerness to welcome some newcomer to their hallowed halls. Because, of course, she wanted to give the girl a warm and cheery Haven High welcome.

As if.

"Ms. Grace, you're late!" called the school secretary, catching Harper wandering slowly down the hall and hauling her back into the office. "Come in, come in! Meet Haven High's newest student."

Squirming out of Mrs. Schlegel's greasy grip, Harper put on her best good-girl smile. It never hurt to curry some favor with the school's high and mighty (or their secretaries), and besides, a new student was something to see. Something new and different—and there was very little at Haven High that was ever new or different. She just hoped this one wouldn't turn out to be as big a loser as the last new girl had been. Heidi Kluger. A fat girl's name, Harper supposed—she shouldn't have been too surprised. But today—

"Harper Grace, meet Kaia. Kaia Sellers, Haven High's newest senior." Mrs. Schlegel beamed at the two girls, as if expecting their lifelong friendship to begin immediately. "Kaia, Harper will be showing you around today. I'm sure she'll be happy to give you all the 411 you need."

Harper barely noticed the secretary's pathetic attempt to co-opt some teen "lingo"—she was frozen, staring at the new girl. Who was most definitely not fat. Not ugly. Not a loser.

No, from the BCBG shoes to the Marc Jacobs bag to the Ella Moss top, this girl was definitely a contender. Long, silky black hair, every strand perfectly in place (Harper unconsciously raised a hand to her own wild mane of loose curls). A delicate, china doll face with just a hint of makeup to bring out her deep green eyes and high cheekbones. And the clothes . . . Harper squelched a stab of envy, thinking of the pile of rejects still lying on her bedroom floor. The winning ensemble, hip-hugging jeans and a white backless top (the better to show off her deep tan) had seemed a good choice in the morning, but although she'd driven two hours to Ludlow this summer to find the Diesel knockoffs, she could hardly call them haute couture. Faux couture, maybe. No one around here could tell the difference. But this girl—in a red silk printed halter and matching red Max Mara skirt, an outfit Harper was sure she'd spotted in last month's *Cosmo*—this girl looked like she could.

Trying her best not to imagine what the arrival of this

cooler-than-thou girl might do to her carefully maintained social status, Harper took a deep breath and began the tour. She led Kaia (what kind of a name was that, anyway?) down the hall, furiously searching for something to say that would make her sound more sophisticated than the small-town hick Kaia was sure to be expecting.

But, wit and charm failing her when she needed them the most, Harper settled for the obvious.

"So, where are you from?"

"Oh, around," Kaia said, looking bored. "We have an apartment in New York—and my mother keeps a place in the country. Of course, some years I'm away at school. . . ."

Boarding school? Harper fought to maintain a neutral expression—just because the new girl was the epitome of urban rich cool and looked as if she'd just walked off a movie screen was no reason to panic.

And maybe . . .

Maybe Little Miss Perfect would actually be an asset. There had to be a way.

"Boarding school?" Harper asked, trying to sound as if she cared—though not too much, of course. "So what happened?"

"Which school?" asked Kaia, smirking. "This last time? Long story. Let's just say that if you're going to be sneaking two guys out your window, it's best to check first that the headmistress isn't spending the evening in the quad, watching a meteor shower. It's also probably best if the guys aren't carrying a stash of pot—the other half of which is in your dorm room."

Harper burst into laughter. If nothing else, this was going to be interesting.

"So as punishment, they exiled you to no-man's-land?"

"Yeah, my dad lives out here. Tough love, right? I guess they figured there'd be no trouble for me to get into out in the middle of nowhere." Kaia, who had been smiling, suddenly frowned and looked around her. "Obviously, they were right."

It was true. Haven High wasn't much to look at—and appearances weren't deceiving. The squat building, erected in the late sixties, had been ahead of its time, its designers embracing the riot-proof concrete bunker style of architecture that grew so popular in the next decade and then deservedly vanished from sight. It was an ugly and impersonal structure, painted long ago in shades of rust and mud—also, conveniently, the school colors (although the powers that be preferred to refer to them as orange and brown). Built to accommodate a town swelled by baby boomers, the small school now housed an even smaller student body, and the dilapidated hallway in which Kaia and Harper stood was largely empty.

The girls fell silent for a moment, contemplating the peeling paint, the faint scent of cleaning fluid mixed with mashed potatoes drifting over from the cafeteria. The year to come. At the moment, neither was too thrilled by the prospect.

"So, Harper Grace," Kaia began, breaking the awkward moment. "I don't suppose that's any relation to Grace, California, my oh-so-fabulous new hometown?"

"You got it," Harper replied, allowing herself a modest smile. She did love being great-great-great-granddaddy's little girl. "Grace Mines, Grace Library, Grace, CA. There used to be a Grace High School, too, but it burned down in the fifties."

Kaia failed to look impressed—or even particularly

interested. But Harper persevered. "This used to be a mining town, you know. My great-great-great-grandfather was like a king around here. Graces ran the mine all the way until it closed in the forties."

"Uh-huh."

Of course, Harper didn't mention the fact that a few years after the mine ran dry, the family bank account had done the same. Being a Grace somehow didn't seem to mean as much these days when the only family business was a dry cleaning shop on North Hampton Street. But at least she had the name.

Not that Kaia seemed to care.

What was the point of trying to impress this girl, anyway? She'd find out soon enough that Harper was as good as it got around here. When that happened, she'd come crawling back—in the meantime, why bother trying?

And with that, Harper reverted to autopilot tour guide mode.

"And this is the gym," she explained, directing Kaia's attention to the wall moldings. "Refurbished in 1979, it can hold over one hundred people . . ."

You think you're bored now, Kaia? she thought. *You ain't seen nothing yet.*

"She said *what?*" Miranda's eyes widened.

Harper grinned. She so loved a good story, and Miranda was such an appreciative audience—suitably shocked and awed in all the right places. Not that that was why Harper kept her around, of course . . . but it didn't hurt.

"You heard me. I asked her why she'd been kicked out

of her swanky boarding school and that's what she told me."
Feigning sudden disinterest in Kaia's sleazy past, Harper idly
picked up one of the beakers of solution sitting on the lab
table in front of her—but, thinking better of it, quickly set
it down again. As if she'd been paying attention to what
they were supposed to be doing with all this stuff.

Miranda let out a long, low whistle. "Do you think it's
true?"

Harper shrugged.

"Who knows. To be honest, she looked like she'd lie
about her own name if she thought it would get a rise out
of people. You know the type."

Miranda arched an eyebrow but said nothing.

"What?" Harper asked.

Miranda looked at her pointedly.

"Remind you of anyone you know?" she asked finally.

"Who, me?" Harper answered, forcing a laugh—and
ignoring the annoying ring of truth. "In her dreams,
maybe. You should have seen her, sauntering around like
she owns the place, acting like I'm going to collapse in awe
of her Marc Jacobs bag."

"*Marc Jacobs?*"

"Oh God, chill out." The shock and awe reactions were
suddenly getting a little old. "It was just a bag. I'm sure it
was a fake. You can always tell."

Must have been. Harper's "Kate Spade" bag looked real
from a distance too. But it wasn't. Obviously.

But Miranda wouldn't be put off the scent. "So why
do you think that—"

"Girls, a little less conversation, a little more science,
please?"

Mrs. Bonner, a short, all-too-perky blonde who liked to wear her unnecessary white lab coat even on trips to the grocery store (and Harper and Miranda could vouch for this, having once spotted the white-smocked figure ferrying a case of Budweiser out of the Shop 'n' Save), shot them a warning look and continued pacing around the room.

They were supposed to be titrating their solvent—or dissolving their titration, or something along those lines, Harper couldn't remember. Yet another reason, come to think of it, that it was useful to keep Miranda around. That and the fact that they'd been best friends since the third grade, when Mikey Mandel had knocked over their care-fully constructed LEGO tower and Harper had punched him in the stomach. Mikey wasn't too happy—and Miranda had stuck by her side through all the hair-pulling, pinching, wrestling, and screaming that followed, through the unsuc-cessful lying and excuses when they'd been caught by the recess monitor, through the long hours they'd spent sitting out in the hall "thinking about their actions." Nine years later, Miranda had grown (if not as many inches as she'd hoped) from a shy, scrawny tomboy into a smart, snarky girl with a killer smile and the quickest wit in the West, and she was still loyally cleaning up Harper's messes—or, when that failed, readily plunging after her into the mud. Mikey Mandel, on the other hand, had grown into a serious stud: six foot four, football team's star running back, scruffy hair, smoldering eyes, never without a smiling blonde on his arm—and he was still a prick.

"I can't believe she's actually making us do a *lab* on the first day of school," Harper complained, digging through the photocopied packet of instructions, searching for some hint of what she was supposed to do with the multicolored liquids staring her down from atop the table. "It's inhuman."

"Who ever said the Bonner was human?" Miranda asked, carefully suspending their beaker of solution over the lit Bunsen burner.

It was true—they'd had her for science three years in a row (nothing ever changed at Haven High), and in all that time she'd yet to show up with new hair, new shoes, or a new lab coat—and who could imagine what lay beneath the glorified white sheet? Their very own Frankenstein's Monster, for all Harper knew. Maybe their science teacher was just some student's award-winning science project. She stifled a laugh at the thought.

"What?" hissed Miranda, flashing her a look of caution as the teacher circled toward them again. They bent intently over their flasks and beakers, feigning enthusiasm in the scientific process. The two girls at the next table squealed with joy as they measured their solvent—just as they'd predicted, to the millimeter. Woo-hoo.

"Great job, Einstein," Harper grumbled to the nearest squealer, a loser in a loose polo shirt and dark-rimmed glasses whom she recognized vaguely from homeroom. Probably on the math team. Or the chess "squad." "Can you invent a chemical solution that will make us care?"

The girl and her equally geeky lab partner studiously ignored her—but at least they shut up. Harper knew she probably shouldn't alienate anyone who might later be persuaded to do her work for her (since she knew from experience that doing these labs herself was basically a no-go), but it was all just too tempting. Especially given the mood she was in: shitty.

"So, is she going to be here all year?" Miranda whispered, once Bonner was a safe distance away.

"Who? Marie Curie over there? I hope not. I've already got a headache."

"No, the new girl—Kaia? How long's she staying?"

Harper shrugged. She was already sorry she'd ever started this conversation—she didn't want to talk about the new girl anymore, especially since this was shaping up to be the start of a yearlong conversation.

"It's a little hot and stuffy in here, don't you think?" she asked, dodging Miranda's question.

"What? I guess. So?"

"So maybe it's time we get a little fresh air." Before Miranda could stop her, Harper crumpled up a piece of paper, dipped it into the Bunsen burner's flame for a moment, and then surreptitiously tossed the fiery ball into their trash can.

"What the hell are you doing?" Miranda hissed.

Harper ignored her, and instead watched with triumph and delight as flames began to lick at the edges of the squat trash can, slowly consuming the small collection of crumpled paper. It was mesmerizing.

"Fire!" Harper finally shouted.

On cue, the girls next to her began squealing in horror, and one slammed her fist into the emergency sprinkler button that hung next to each lab table.

And that was all it took.

The room began to rain.

The smoke alarm blared.

And chaos broke out as the roomful of students scrambled to get their stuff together and escape the downpour, pushing and shoving each other out of the way, only a couple of them craning their necks to search for the fire, which had very quickly gone out. Mrs. Bonner raced back and forth across the room, herding students out of danger but clearly more concerned about making sure that her precious chemicals and lab equipment stayed safe, sound, and dry.

Laughing, water pouring down her face, Harper pulled Miranda out of the classroom and down the hall. They ran for an exit together and ducked into the parking lot, finally sinking down behind a row of parked cars, convulsing with laughter on the warm concrete.

"I can't believe you just did that," Miranda gasped, half annoyed and half amazed. "I'm totally soaked."

Harper grinned lazily and, catlike, stretched her body out and preened in the sun.

"You'll dry. And now instead of titrating and distilling and blah, blah, blah, we can spend the rest of the hour talking about the important things in life."

"Like?"

"I don't know. Guys? What we're going to do this weekend? Whether any of your cigarettes are still dry enough to smoke?"

Sighing, Miranda pulled out her pack—only slightly wet on one corner—and tossed it to Harper.

"I don't want to rain on your parade, but did you even stop to consider what would happen if you'd gotten caught? Or if, I don't know, you'd *set the school on fire?*"

"Rand, it was a *double period.*" Harper spoke slowly and

loudly, as if deciding that Miranda needed a little help trying to wrap her brain around the basics. "We would have been stuck in there *forever*."

"Oh, please," Miranda snorted. She began digging through her soggy backpack, assessing the damage: Spanish notebook: dry. Sort of. Paperback *Hamlet* for AP English: soaked. Stila mascara and MAC lipstick: mercifully intact. "If you'd just waited, we would have been out in an hour."

Harper took a long drag on the cigarette and took a moment to consider that. She shook her head.

"We're seniors now," she said finally. "We've waited long enough."

Boring.

It had taken the girl—Harper—an endless fifty minutes to guide Kaia through the school, fifty minutes of her life that she would never get back. And the rest of the morning had just been more of the same. People she didn't want to meet, telling her things she didn't want to know. As if she cared what to do or where to go in this shoebox of a school, or had any interest in who was who—or who was sleeping with whom—as if the mundane details of anything in this tedious town could be anything less than tedious.

Anything but boring.

Boring.

Boring.

The word had been beating a steady tattoo in her head ever since she'd arrived in this one-horse (or in this case, she supposed, one-Wal-Mart) town. Not by plane, of course. There was no airport in Grace, CA. Apparently, there was no airport anywhere *near* Grace, CA, if the endless drive from Las Vegas was any indication. Though to be honest, she was surprised there were even cars in the ridiculous town—the whole place had the feel of a different century, except for the tacky tourist strip of Route 66 running through the town center—*there* time seemed frozen in a particularly bad year of the 1970s.

She'd plodded through three hours of the school day and knew pretty much all that she needed to know about her new life in Grace—as in, there wasn't going to be much of one. Now here she was, standing in line in a cafeteria—a *cafeteria*, a smelly, cramped room painted hospital green, with long metal tables bolted to the floor, cranky old women in hairnets doling out lumps of food, hordes of dull-eyed students who at least deserved credit for not all outweighing an elephant, if they'd been eating this greasy crap their entire lives. Who knew places like this actually existed? Kaia's schooltime meals had varied. There was the gourmet health food in the regal boarding school dining hall, with its vaulted ceilings and centuries-old oak tables. And of course the Upper West Side takeout cuisine grabbed to go during lunch periods—well, any and all periods—at her city prep school. (Prep school had been before *and* after boarding school—getting kicked out was easy when you had plenty of money and connections to kick you into somewhere else. How was Kaia supposed to know that she would only have so many opportunities to vacillate between the frying pan and fire before getting thrown off the stove altogether?) Even the lunches the maid had occasionally put together for her—or, years ago, the lunches her mother had packed before she'd decided that mothering was too last season—even those had been better than this slop. But that was then, this was now. This was life in Grace: dry heat, neon, decrepit gas stations, incompetent teachers, grease, dust, *cafeterias*. This was her life.

She was stuck. Stranded. A world away from everyone and everything she'd ever known.

At least it was also a world away from her mother. Thank God for small favors, right?

"Kaia, over here!"

Kaia whirled around to see the mind-numbing tour guide, Harper, waving in her direction. She stuck on a smile—though she didn't trust Harper any farther than she could throw her (which, judging from the poorly hidden roll of flesh squeezed into the waistband of the girl's faux designer jeans, wouldn't be very far at all). But no reason to burn any bridges—not yet, at least. Besides, no way was she eating alone.

"Hi, Harper," she said lazily, paying for her "lunch" (an apple, skim milk, and some wilted lettuce masquerading as a salad).

"*My friends* wanted you to come have lunch with us," Harper explained.

Kaia noticed, but didn't mention, the pronoun that was plainly missing from Harper's halfhearted invitation. She followed Harper obediently out of the dingy cafeteria and into the cramped "quad" behind it, where students were apparently allowed to eat—if they could find a place to perch amidst the broken tables, scattered garbage, and ever-present dust. Kaia wrinkled her nose—this whole school should be declared a toxic waste site. Students included.

"Everyone, this is Kaia Sellers," Harper said with a sarcastic flourish of her hands, once they'd found the right table.

Mmm . . . maybe not *all* the students. "Everyone" apparently included two tasty guys who looked as if they'd just walked out of an Abercrombie ad. They were sprawled on the wooden benches along with a few other apparent A-listers—even mahogany-filled dining halls have tables set aside for the social elite, and as a life-long member of that class, Kaia could spot the signs from a mile away. The table was on the outskirts of the quad, far from the lunchroom monitor who poked her head outside every once in a while to make sure no one was smoking, drinking, or destroying school property. But even physically on the margins, the group was still somehow at the center of everything—attention, con-versation, focus. These kids were loved, they were hated—but most of all, they were watched. Kaia knew the feeling.

"Kaia, this is Miranda Stevens." Harper stood next to Kaia but had carefully angled her body away, so that she could keep a close watch on her but didn't have to make any direct eye contact.

One of the girls, apparently Miranda, stepped forward to shake Kaia's hand. Scarecrow thin, limp, dull hair pulled back into geeky braids, some unfortunate fashion choices—the white T-shirt under the imitation Chanel jacket just wasn't doing it. *But cute,* Kaia thought. She'd do.

"And I'm Beth," the other girl, blond and beautiful—if you liked that farmer's daughter thing—waved from the other end of the table, where she was nuzzled under the arm of Abercrombie Number One. "Welcome to Haven High. I'm sure you—"

"And this is Adam and Kane," Harper interrupted,

stepping around to the other side of the table and placing a possessive hand on each of their backs. Adam was an all-American boy, with blond hair, a square jaw, an honest face, a dark blue T-shirt that no doubt hid washboard abs but revealed astonishingly thick biceps—no surprise, then, that he would be dating the farmer's daughter, Kaia supposed. He kept one arm tightly around the blond girl, but reached out the other to shake Kaia's hand. His fingers were warm, his grasp firm—she held it just a second too long.

Kane, on the other hand—there was nothing honest about him. The same muscles (they definitely didn't make them like this in New York), the same striking good looks, but she could tell from his hooded eyes, from the smirk playing across his lips, from his unabashed and appreciative appraisal of her body as he rose to greet her, that he was playing in a different league. Maybe playing a different game.

Again Kaia extended a hand; instead of shaking it, Kane gently turned it face down, then raised it to his lips and gave it a light kiss.

"Charmed," he said. From anyone else, it might have been smarmy. From him? It worked.

Both boys grinned at her, and Kaia could feel their gazes traveling down her long neck and lingering at the point where her silver pendant disappeared into the darkness of her low-cut V-neck. *Boys and cleavage,* she thought. *It never fails.*

She also noticed Harper noticing the boys' glances—and saw the girl's eyes narrow.

Not bad, Kaia decided. Pretty standard, maybe, but not too bad.

Who knows—maybe she could have a little fun here after all. . . .

It was a perverse rule of nature: The first day of school always lasted forever. Temporal distortion not covered by the theory of relativity: One hour of first-day time roughly equivalent to half an eternity of normal time. Endless minutes of staring out the window, cursing the wasted daylight, all that time *not* getting a tan, *not* drinking a frozen strawberry margarita, *not* listening to cheesy eighties music and complaining there was never anything to do while secretly delighting in the Madonna sing-along. Outside was suddenly Eden—inside, sweating through sixth period and watching the decrepit clock tick off the minutes, surely nothing less than the seventh level of Hell.

But this year, waiting through the day presented, at least for some, a special torture. They weren't waiting for the final bell, they were waiting for the final period: advanced French. Normally a snoozefest with 150-year-old Madame Marshak (who, in the best tradition of hatefully eccentric high school French teachers, remained convinced of her essential Frenchness, despite her Houston birth certificate and unmistakable Texan twang). But this year Marshak had finally gone on to greener pastures—her sister's house in Buffalo. Although given her advanced age and penchant for driving around tipsy after too much cheap French wine, it seemed likely that Buffalo would be only a brief layover on the way to her final destination.

Regardless, there was a new *professeur* in town—the first new teacher Haven High had seen in years.

He was young.

He was British.

And, if freshman gossip was to be believed—for he'd already made an appearance in third period's French for annoying beginners—he was hot.

Seriously hot.

There was only one advanced French class, which meant that Beth, Harper, and now Kaia would be stuck in the small room together all year long. Beth sat toward the front (though not in the front row—she'd learned long ago that good grades were one thing, teacher's pet was quite another) and flipped through her organizer, trying to figure out how she was going to fit in homework, editing the school newspaper, applying to colleges, babysitting her little brothers, and working a part-time job without going insane. And, oh yeah, without letting her boyfriend forget what she looked like.

Harper, ensconced as usual in the back row, lazily examined her nails and decided that it was definitely time for a manicure. And, come to think of it, maybe a pedicure. And a haircut. Not that there was a decent salon anywhere in town, but at Betty's off of Green Street, they did a slightly better than half-assed job, and threw in a ten-minute head and shoulder massage for free. Which was an appealing thought—it was only the first day of school and already she could use a serious de-stressing.

Kaia slipped into the classroom just before the bell— Haven High stuck its language classes down in the basement, and she'd already stumbled across a decrepit boiler room and overstuffed janitor's closet before finally finding her way here. She took the only seat that was left, on the aisle next to a boy who smelled like rotten fruit. A fitting end to the day. Or *un fin parfait pour le jour*, as her new French teacher would say. Wherever he was. "Advanced" French. Such a waste of her time, Kaia thought, considering she'd spent half of last summer on the Riviera, gossiping with the château's staff like a native. Such a joke. Such a—

Such an unexpected treat. If the man who had just appeared in the doorway, flashed the class a rakish smile, ran a hand through his adorably floppy hair, and strode to the front of the room was actually their teacher, life at Haven High was suddenly looking up.

For the rumors were right.

This guy was hot.

Seriously hot.

Just like a movie star, Beth sighed to herself as he grabbed a piece of chalk and wrote his name on the board in quick, loping script.

Jack Powell.

"Hola! Me llamo Jack Powell. Como esta?" he asked, as the class stared blankly back at him. "Okay, and if you understood any of that, you're probably in the wrong place and you should get out. As for the rest of you, *bienvenue* and welcome to French 4."

Hot and British, Harper mused. *Tasty—Hugh Grant meets Clive Owen. So what the hell is he doing here?*

"As you probably know, I'm new around here," Powell admitted, taking off his sports jacket and perching casually on the edge of his desk. "So I'm sure this class is going to have some surprises to offer all of us."

You have no idea, Kaia thought. She had never expected

to find someone like him—so handsome, so charming, so cosmopolitan, so *her*—in this shitty town. But now that opportunity had knocked, it seemed only polite to open the door and invite him in.

chapter

3

"Adam, I told you. Not yet." Beth reached out a hand toward him, but he pulled away, rolling over on his side. It was still strange for her to see him there, in the bed she'd slept in since she was a child. It was still a child's room, really—ruffled bedspread, white wooden furniture with light blue trim, so much pink that it was embarrassing. If she'd had her way, the room would be sophisticated and sparse, with only a dark mahogany desk, some Ansel Adams prints on the wall, and a crowded bookshelf in the corner. But these days her parents had neither the money nor the patience for interior decorating, so her seventeen-year-old self was forever trapped in the pink pleated land of her eight-year-old self's dreams. There was even a stuffed animal, the only thing in the room she didn't hate—though at the moment, poor Snuffy the Turtle was crushed beneath Adam's half-naked body. *One of these things is not like the other,* she thought crazily, the Sesame Street lyric wandering through her mind as she sought frantically for something to say that would make Adam understand. Was this really her life? "I'm just not ready."

"I know, and I'm not trying to rush you," he said with his back to her, a petulant tone creeping into his voice. "I'm *not*—it's just that . . ."

Beth sat up and pulled on her pale pink bra, struggling to fasten the clasp behind her. It was past five and her mother would be home soon. Now was not the time for this conversation—couldn't he see that?

"Look, Adam, you know it's not that I don't love you, it's not that I don't want to . . ." God, how she wanted to!

"What, then?" He rolled back to face her, clasping her hands and pulling her close. "What's stopping us? I know you wanted to wait . . . but . . . what are we waiting for?"

If only she knew the answer. If only she could put into words the heart-stopping terror she felt when she let her fantasies get away from her and imagined throwing herself at him, losing herself to the moment, and—but her imagination took her only so far. That's when the terror set in. And however handsome he looked lying there, one arm stretched out over his head and a lock of hair falling over his deep, dark eyes, however much she may have wanted him—all of him—she just couldn't do it. Not yet. Not like this.

It hadn't always been like this, the pressure, the silent give-and-take, worrying about what she wanted and what he wanted and what happened next. No, in the beginning, it had been simple. She had hated him.

Totally hated him, and everything he stood for—which as far as she was concerned, was sports, sex, and beer. She'd hated the way the whole school thought he walked on water, just because he could swim quickly across a pool every fall, could drop a ball into a hoop every winter, just because he was tall, and chiseled, and had a smile that warmed you like the sun. She'd hated his stupid jock clothes, his stupid jock jokes—most of all, his stupid jock friends, and the girls who hung all over them. The guys were all so arrogant, acting like they governed the school, like Beth and her friends were expected to bow and curtsy every time they swept down the hall—and the girls were even worse, simpering and giggling, desperately trying to keep their jock's attention, or at least to win favor with Harper and her gang, the female counterpart to all this athletic royalty.

When she'd been stuck with Adam as a lab partner last year in bio, all her friends had been jealous—but Beth had just sighed in exhaustion, already figuring that she'd have to do all the work. And she'd been right—put a scalpel in his hands and a pickled frog on a slab in front of him, and Adam was as incompetent and helpless as she would be if plopped down in the middle of a basketball court, facing down the WNBA all-star team. She'd been right about that—but not much else.

He wasn't arrogant, he wasn't stupid, he wasn't an asshole or a dumb jock. By October he was just . . . Adam. Sweet, funny, adorable—and, for whatever reason, he would stop at nothing until she went out with him. And, for whatever reason—well, basically for the reason that it seemed he'd flirted with or dated half the school, and she didn't particularly want to be his next randomly selected conquest—she refused. And refused again. How many times had she said no?

Too many—but it hadn't stopped him. He'd started

slipping notes in her locker, leaving flowers for her at her seat in lab—he wouldn't give up. And then came the day he'd waited for her at her locker after school, greeting her with a giddy smile and a goofy wave. Before she knew it, he was down on one knee.

"Marry me?" he'd asked, pulling a giant plastic ring out of his pocket. It was a bright blue flower, about the size of her palm. It was ludicrous—and irresistible.

"Get up!" she'd urged him through her giggles, blushing furiously as a crowd began to gather.

"Not until you give me a chance," he had sworn, seemingly oblivious to the curiosity-seekers. Or maybe he was just used to being the center of attention.

"I'm not marrying you, idiot," she'd laughed, tugging at his arm. "Come on, get up!"

But he had stayed in position. "Okay then, we'll start slow. One date—one chance. Then I'll never bother you again."

How could she say no?

He'd been her first kiss, her first boyfriend, her first love, her first—everything. He'd been so patient, so tender, so gentle, and everything had been wonderful. Perfect. Until now—when she wanted him more than ever, and it only made things worse. And suddenly everything that had been easy between them, all the effortless conversation, the casual kisses, the laughter—it was all weighed down by the silence of what they never said, what they couldn't talk about. Everything on the surface was still so right—but beneath that, Beth feared, there was something brittle, something fragile. Something wrong.

She leaned over and kissed him gently on the forehead

and once on the lips, then hopped out of bed to gather up the clothes they'd strewn haphazardly across her bedroom.

"Up 'n' Adam," she chirped, hoping her voice wasn't shaking. She tossed a balled-up T-shirt toward him. "You know my mother will be home any minute, and if she finds us up here . . ."

Silently, Adam got out of bed and pulled on his clothes. The quiet minutes dragged on for an eternity, until Beth was afraid he would leave without saying another word. But before he did, he came up and put his arms around her, pulling her into a tight embrace. Beth buried her head in his chest, reveling in the soft, familiar scent of his cologne and trying her best to fight back the tears.

"You know I love you," he whispered. He released her, then tipped her chin up, forcing her to meet his eyes. "You know I love you," he said again, his lips only a breath away. "And you know I'll wait."

Beth nodded. She knew he loved her, and she knew he would wait—but for how long?

Kane surveyed the tacky surroundings in disgust. Magazine clippings from the fifties papered the walls, fake plastic records dangled from the ceiling, and a giant neon jukebox blasted out oldies while bored waitresses plodded back and forth between the crowded booths and the crowded kitchen, snapping their gum and pretending they didn't desperately wish they were somewhere, anywhere, else.

"Remind me again why we keep coming back here?" he asked.

Harper hit an imaginary *Jeopardy!* buzzer.

"What is 'the only diner in town'?" she reminded him.

She took another spoonful of her ice-cream sundae and moaned with pleasure. "Besides, who could deny the appeal of a restaurant with a motto like that?" She tapped a perfectly manicured finger on top of the fluorescent menu: LIFE IS SHORT—EAT DESSERT FIRST.

"Good point," Kane admitted, scooping off a good chunk of her ice cream, complete with cherry—he'd finished his own sundae within minutes of its arrival.

"Hands off!" Harper laughed, smacking his spoon away. "Sure you don't want some, Miranda?" she asked, pushing the giant bowl across the table toward her friend. Miranda squirmed back, waving it away.

"Some of us actually want to have room for dinner," she pointed out.

"Oh, come on, Miranda, live a little," Kane encouraged her, grabbing a spoon and digging in once again. "Be a rebel—I know you've got some bad girl blood in there somewhere."

Miranda hesitantly took a small bite of the ice cream, flushing as his deep chocolate eyes paused on her and a slow, satisfied smile lit up his face.

"Atta girl. I knew you had it in you."

Is he flirting *with me?* she wondered.

If only.

Miranda had known Kane for almost as long as she'd known Harper (and, basically, everyone else in this town)—a few minutes short of forever. She doubted that he remembered the time they'd spent a third grade recess playing dominoes together, or the knight in shining armor moment when he'd tossed her a towel after an embarrassing "wardrobe malfunction" at Shayna Hernandez's eighth grade pool party. In fact, she doubted that he would even remember her name—or at least admit to doing so—if she wasn't usually joined at the hip with Harper, one of the only people that Kane didn't find to be a yawn a minute. But whatever the reason that put him across the table from her so often, she was grateful. And sometimes wondered whether this wasn't perhaps the year that he'd get sick of the bimbos and finally notice her. A girl could dream, couldn't she?

Besides, thanks to Harper's intervention and some—okay, a lot of—careful dieting, she now had much better hair, clothes, and body than she'd had in eighth grade. Maybe the next time her bikini top popped off, Kane wouldn't be so quick with the towel. . . .

"Earth to Miranda," his voice punctured her reverie. "Dreaming about my hot bod again? You girls just can't help yourselves, can you?"

Miranda snorted, hoping her face wasn't too red. "As if."

Did she sound believably casual—but not so disgusted that he would think it inconceivable that she'd been thinking about his tightly toned forearms?

Miranda knew there was a middle ground somewhere between obsessed stalker and mortal enemy, but she'd never had much luck finding it. (This likely explained why all her carefully constructed flirty banter, designed to make junior high crush Rob Schwartz realize she was interested, but not *too* interested, had instead left the JV quarterback with the unshakeable conviction that she hated him.)

She'd gotten a little better since then—but not much.

Beth and Adam were late.

They came into the diner arm in arm, whispering to each other. Harper waved to get their attention, then quickly looked away. It was too sickening to watch.

"Where've you guys been?" Kane asked with a leer when they arrived at the table. "As if I have to ask."

Beth tucked her hair behind her ears, blushing, and Adam began to stammer out something about lost keys and car trouble and—

"Oh, just sit down," Harper interrupted. "We waited for you to order dinner, and we're starving, so let's just get to it."

"Spoken with your usual grace and accuracy," Kane said. "I second the motion."

Beth and Adam squeezed into the booth next to Miranda, smushing her up against the window, since the bench was meant for only two people. But Harper chose not to say anything about it—the way things were going, Beth would probably just smile politely and offer to spend the rest of the night perched on Adam's lap, to save room. She was just *so* accommodating. And, Harper had to admit, beautiful. She'd changed out of her first-day-of-school outfit (standard Beth: classic-cut jeans, black T-shirt, gold hoop earrings, bland and forgettable) into a backless turquoise sundress that matched her eyes and perfectly set off her sun-drenched hair. And Harper wasn't the only one to appreciate it. As Beth leaned forward to order her food, Adam reached over and began slowly rubbing her bare back; Harper couldn't pull her eyes away from his hand, lightly playing its way up and down Beth's skin. She could almost feel its warm pressure on her own.

Harper shook her head violently to knock the fantasy away, and then waved them all to be quiet. There was a reason she'd invited them out tonight—aside from the understandable need for large amounts of grease and sugar after the long first day of school. And, since she was losing her appetite by the minute watching the lovebirds fawn, it was probably time to get started.

"Okay, now that you're *all* here"—she tried not to glare at Beth—"here's the deal. We've got two weeks until the annual lame back-to-school formal, right?"

Kane groaned. "Don't remind me. What a joke."

Harper ignored him and continued. "And two weeks until the annual top secret after party, organized by a select group of seniors."

"Kerry Stanton and those girls did it last year, right?" Beth asked. "Wonder who they tapped for this year."

Harper gave her a withering stare. Was the girl an idiot?

"Kerry e-mailed me this afternoon," Harper explained with a self-satisfied grin. "Looks like I'm up."

"You?" Miranda asked, grinning. "Awesome."

"Actually—us."

Adam held up his hands in protest. "Hold up, Harper—look, we're all impressed that you're now officially the coolest of the cool and all, but if you think you're roping me into some kind of *dance* committee . . ."

"God, it's not a dance, Adam. It's a party. A secret, illicit, just-for-seniors party?" She smiled winningly. "And I know you *all* want to help out, get on the inside track, be adored by the masses—"

"Not to mention, get first dibs on the best beer and the comfiest mattresses," Kane pointed out. "Sign me up."

Harper smacked him and was about to launch back into her spiel when the diner door opened, and in walked Kaia. On anyone else, her Little Black Dress would have looked ridiculously out of place amidst the neon and trucker chic, but Kaia seemed oblivious of context, striding forward with purpose and grace as if, to her, the waitresses appeared clad in Hugo Boss, not polyester. She looked completely at ease, though Harper could tell, just from the little things—the single finger she'd used to push open the door as if afraid of the germs, the delicate steps she took as if expecting at any moment to splash her kitten heel into a puddle of mustard—that she was not.

"Are you kidding me?" Harper muttered to herself. "Maybe she won't see—"

"Kaia, over here!" Beth chirped, waving the new girl over. "I invited her to come along," she explained to the table. "I thought it would be nice—you know, she doesn't know anyone, and—what?" she asked, irritated, as the boys laughed, while Miranda and Harper just rolled their eyes. "What is it?"

"It was a nice thing to do," Adam assured her, laying a hand on hers. "I'm sure she appreciated it."

"I know *I* do," Kane added, quickly shutting up as Kaia approached.

"Am I too late?" Kaia asked as she arrived at the table, eyeing the empty ice-cream dishes.

"No, we haven't even ordered yet," Kane reassured her, shifting over to make room for her (now Harper too was smushed against the window—and if there was going to be a male body pressed up against her like this, Kane's was really *not* the one she would have chosen). "Don't worry, Harper just likes to eat dessert first."

"Why am I not surprised?" Kaia asked, and while her tone was light and pleasant, Harper could feel the girl's icy eyes boring through her.

"So, about this party . . ." Miranda began, trying to defuse the tension.

Harper kicked her furiously under the table, but it was too late.

"Party?" Kaia asked. "Sounds like I'm just in time."

"We're all going to help Harper organize this party thing in a couple of weeks," Adam explained.

What was with the "we"? Harper wondered. He hadn't sounded so enthused a moment ago. Before *she* walked in.

"Not all of us," Beth added, her eyes darting away. "Sorry, Harper, I wish I could help, but I'm way too busy already."

"What are you talking about?" Adam asked. He whirled to face her, his mouth crinkling into a frown.

"You know, I have a bunch of after-school meetings, and this new job, and my brothers to take care of, and—"

"Can't you just make the time? We never get to do anything like this *together*," he complained, running a hand through his hair in frustration. He took her hand in his, but she quickly pulled it away.

"No, I can't just *make* time—it's not that easy. And anyway—" Beth suddenly realized that the whole table was eagerly watching their back-and-forth. "Can we just talk about this later?" she requested in a more measured tone.

"Fine. Whatever," Adam said sulkily. "I guess Kaia can take your spot."

"I'm sure Kaia's way too busy for that sort of thing,"

Harper quickly interrupted. "Places to go, people to do, you know how it is."

"Harper!" Adam turned toward her, shocked.

"What? She's a big-city girl—why would she want to waste her time on small-town shit like this?"

"Uh, she is sitting right here, you know," Kaia pointed out. "Though apparently you'd prefer it if I weren't. Excuse me." And, perfectly composed, she stood up and glided toward the door.

"What the hell are you doing?" Adam hissed. "Why are you acting like this?"

"Whatever, she said it herself this morning," Harper told him. She raised her voice so that more of the restaurant—specifically, those who were putting on a big show of leaving in a petty snit—could hear her. "All she cares about are drugs and sex."

"Which should give the two of you a lot in common," Adam retorted, and pushed himself away from the table, following Kaia out of the restaurant.

Harper sucked in her breath sharply, and the rest of them stared at her in stunned silence. It was a pretty rare sight to see perpetually good-natured Adam turn ugly—and an even rarer one to see Harper as the target of his attack. Harper squirmed under their gazes and chewed nervously on the inside of her cheek. Picking a fight with Adam wasn't part of tonight's plans—but then again, having Kaia tag along with the whole party planning thing wasn't either. There had been a brief, blessed moment, just after Beth had refused to play, when Harper imagined what it might be like, working side by side with Adam—long hours, private strategy sessions, laughter, flirting, and then one day, maybe, she would make her move. Or—even better—he would make his. One moment. And then Kaia had ruined everything.

Adam soon led Kaia back into the restaurant, his hand held lightly on her back as he guided her down the aisle and back to the table. As Kaia whispered something in his ear and Adam burst into quiet laughter, Harper was hit with a bizarre flash of déjà vu. Hadn't this scene just happened, with a different starlet playing the role of female ingenue? She wondered if Beth, too, had picked up on the instant replay—then again, Miss Manners really had no one to blame but herself, since she was the one who'd invited the wolf to come have dinner with the lambs.

Not that Harper had any intention of playing the lamb in this little romantic grudge match.

Adam and Kaia sat down again, and Harper—after a stern look from Adam—grudgingly apologized. They ate in relative peace, but when the burgers, fries, and Miranda's salad were gone, no one was in the mood for a second round of desserts.

As they rose to leave, Adam pulled Harper aside, and they walked slowly, out of earshot of the rest of the group.

"I'm sorry," he said quietly. "For what I said earlier."

"Don't worry about it," Harper told him, not quite meeting his eyes.

"No, I was totally out of line—it's just, I'm just a little edgy these days." They had reached the door, and Adam held it open and swept her through with exaggerated chivalry. She paused in the doorway and looked up at him, his face only inches away. If she stood on her toes, she'd be close enough to . . . well, it was close. She could smell his cologne, a cool, fresh scent that smelled like rain. Like Adam.

"Seriously, don't worry about it." Harper swallowed her pain and her anger and forced a smile, then gave him a quick kiss on the cheek. "I swear—all is forgiven."

She glared at Kaia's back, a few steps ahead.

Forgiven—but not forgotten.

Kaia took one last disgusted look at the Nifty Fifties Diner before following the "gang" into the parking lot. This town was pathetic. It was like being trapped in the Vegas stage version of a *Dawson's Creek* episode—disgustingly earnest teenagers with boring middle-America issues, prancing around on a set lifted from a Travel Channel rundown of America's Tackiest Tourist Traps. At least there was some good scenery to look at along the way. Exhibit A: Adam Morgan.

"You need a ride, Kaia?" he asked, taking Beth's hand as they headed toward his car, a maroon Chevrolet with a dented fender and a discolored side panel that seemed lifted from a different car.

Kaia, who had parked her father's Mustang around the corner, figured that she could find a way to retrieve it in the morning. Her father was, big shock, out of town—but there were plenty of other cars and people to use. If the maid didn't have time to run her into town in the Beamer, then the gardener could do it in the Audi. Not a problem.

"Actually, I was just about to ask," Kaia answered, smiling at Adam. "I got a ride here from my dad, but he's out for the night—are you sure it's not too much trouble? I live pretty far out."

Beth laughed and jabbed her boyfriend in the arm good-naturedly. "Are you kidding? Adam loves to drive, don't you? I think he secretly wishes I lived out in the middle of nowhere so that he'd have more chances to take his prized possession for a real ride."

Kaia grinned naughtily at the thought of taking Adam for "a real ride," but she kept her mouth shut—it was just too easy. Besides, she'd already committed herself to playing the wounded good girl role. Her little chat with Adam earlier had convinced her that he was just burning for a chance to play knight in shining armor to some fragile princess. And Kaia was happy to accommodate him— which meant the knee-jerk sex kitten comments would just have to go unspoken.

"Great," she said, trying her best not to wrinkle her nose at the sight of Adam's Chevy. It looked even more wretched close up, like a junk heap molded into the shape of a car, held together with duct tape. Prized possession? It didn't speak very well for his taste—of course, from what she'd seen so far, neither did Beth. But she was willing to give him the benefit of the doubt.

She looked over her shoulder at Kane, who was climbing into a vintage silver Camaro. And he was just as hot as Adam, though he lacked the adorable Southern accent. But the guy was obviously a total player—and thus not nearly as much fun to play with. No, she decided, climbing into the backseat and slamming the door shut behind her, Adam it is. At least for now.

Beth and Adam chattered together in the front while Kaia sat in silence, watching the dark streets fly by.

"You want to come back to my place?" Adam asked his

girlfriend. "My mom's probably out for the night. . . ."

There was a long pause, and Beth looked over her shoulder and glanced at Kaia. "I've got a lot of work to do," she said eventually. "And, you know, curfew."

"I just thought that—"

"Why don't you drop me off first," Beth cut him off. "I'm on the way."

Trouble in paradise? Kaia wondered. Interesting.

Adam just grunted and turned off onto a side street. He pulled up in front of a squat ranch house, sandwiched between a row of identically impersonal boxes. A tricycle lay on its side in the middle of the small front lawn, which looked as if it hadn't seen a lawn mower in years. The cramped patch of overgrown weeds was the perfect companion to the house itself, with its peeling paint job and rusted aluminum siding. Home sweet home.

Adam turned off the car and unfastened his seat belt, but Beth stopped him with a quick kiss.

"You don't have to walk me in," she whispered. "I'll just see you tomorrow." She kissed him again, this time long and hard, and then got out of the car and raced up the front walkway, a narrow path of loose gravel and chipped cement. She paused in the doorway, fumbling in her purse for the key, then, finally, pulled open the door and slipped into the house, the slim beam of light cut off as she closed the door behind her.

Adam was still for a moment, watching her figure disappear into the darkness. Then he twisted around in his seat and grinned at Kaia.

"Why don't you come sit up here?" he suggested, patting the seat next to him.

Perfect. Kaia hopped out of the car and switched into the front seat. As she fastened her seat belt, she lightly brushed his hand, which rested on the gearshift—he tensed, almost imperceptibly, and she knew he'd felt the same electric charge of excitement that she had at the touch.

She ignored it, however, and began playing with the radio stations, searching in vain for something that was neither country-and-western nor fire-and-brimstone.

"Not much to listen to out here, is there?" Kaia complained, as Adam started the car and pulled back out onto the road. She flicked the stereo off in disgust. "Not much to do, either."

"No," he admitted. "But it's a good town. Good people, you know?"

Could this guy be any more of an all-American cliché? She didn't know they *made* them like this in real life.

"Anyway," he continued awkwardly, "I'm sorry again about before, in the diner—Harper's just, well . . ."

"An acquired taste?" Kaia suggested, faking a smile.

"I guess you could say that," Adam admitted. "See, the thing you've got to understand about Harper is . . ." His voice faded off, and he squinted his eyes in concentration, trying to find the right words.

"Her bark is worse than her bite?" Kaia offered.

Adam laughed ruefully and shook his head. "No, I'd watch out for her bite, too."

Good to know, Kaia thought. "Then what?" she persisted. "I mean, you seem like such a nice, genuine guy, and I guess I'm just surprised that you're . . . that not all of your friends are . . . I'm just a little surprised." Kaia guessed there was no particularly polite way to say, *So, your friend is an überbitch.*

Hopefully she'd made her point without doing major damage to her mission.

"Look, I know Harper can be kind of—"

"Harsh?"

"Kind of a bitch, basically," Adam acknowledged. Kaia suppressed her laughter—good to know he wasn't totally blind. "It's not something I love about her," Adam continued with a sigh. "But the thing about Harper is, well, things come pretty easy for her. She gets bored—and you can see why."

"Bored? In this town? *No*," Kaia drawled sarcastically. How could you be bored when the bowling alley was open 24/7?

"No, it's not just that," Adam clarified. "It's not just that it's a small town. It's Harper—she just—doesn't belong here, somehow. She's better than this place." He shook his head ruefully. "And the problem is, she knows it."

"It sounds like you—" But Kaia cut herself off almost as soon as she began. No reason to put ideas in his head. If he was too dense to figure it out for himself, she certainly wasn't going to help him along.

"I what?" he asked, confused.

"Nothing." Kaia paused, watching the dark shadows of parked cars, deserted buildings, flat, arid land speed by. The emptiness was endless. "Have a lot of respect for her, that's all," she finished feebly.

"Well, I've known her a long time," he explained, pulling onto the empty highway. "She was the first friend I made when I moved here. I trust her—and whatever else she's done, she's never betrayed that. She's the same with Miranda. When Harper decides you're worthy of her time, she's actually the best friend you could have. Loyal as a pit bull."

"Which would explain both the barking and the biting," Kaia pointed out.

He laughed. "Exactly."

They were both quiet for a moment, and Kaia realized that this was the most she'd ever heard Adam speak. He hadn't said much during dinner, and even when Beth was in the car, he'd mostly been listening to her prattle on about her day. The strong, silent type, Kaia decided. Likes listening better than talking—so maybe she should give him something to listen to.

"Well, pit bull or not, you don't have to worry about me," she assured him. "I can handle myself. You have to be tough when you . . ." She let her voice trail off and looked down at her hands. Would he take the bait?

"When you what?" he asked, sounding concerned.

Score.

"It's just—you know, it's hard, bouncing from school to school, always being the new kid, knowing that neither of your parents want you around. . . ."

Amazing how truth can sometimes be more effective than fiction.

Kaia let her voice tremble, just a bit. "And people assume things about you, you know, treat you in a certain way, like you're this person, this person who has nothing to do with who you really are. . . ."

Adam took one hand off the wheel and rested it on her shoulder; Kaia suppressed a grin.

"Hey, we're not all like that," he assured her.

Kaia laughed, shakily.

"Listen to me, 'poor little rich girl.' And I don't even know you." She wiped an eye, hoping he wouldn't notice the lack of a tear.

"Can we just . . . just forget I said anything?" she asked.

Adam nodded—but he kept a firm hand on her shoulder.

They drove in silence down the empty highway for several miles, until Kaia pointed to the shadowy silhouette of a mailbox, the only sign of civilization along the dark stretch of road.

"Turn up here, I think," she said, and the car swung left, up a long gravel pathway, arriving at the foot of a large house of glass and steel.

"Whoa," Adam murmured softly. "Unbelievable."

The house—more of an estate, really—gleamed in the moonlight. Its sleek modernity would have been utterly out of place amidst the age-encrusted remnants in the Grace town center, but out here on the fringe, the elegant beast seemed a perfect fit with the harsh aesthetics of the dessert landscape. Stark steel beams, giant windows, a jigsaw puzzle of smooth surfaces—it was like no house he'd ever seen.

"This is where you live?" he asked in a hushed voice.

"Like I said, 'poor little rich girl,'" Kaia quipped.

Adam turned off the car and hopped out to open Kaia's door for her.

A total gentleman.

"Listen, Kaia," he said as they walked up the long, narrow path toward her door. "Obviously we don't know each other that well yet, but I just want you to know—if you ever need anyone to talk to, you know, I'm around."

Brushing away another fake tear, Kaia threw her arms around Adam and hugged him tightly to her.

What a body.

"Thank you," she whispered into his ear, making sure to graze his cheek with her moist lips. "You'll never know how much that means to me."

She let herself into the house, pausing in the doorway to watch him walk back to the car. Even his silhouette had sex appeal.

This is almost too easy to be worth my time, she thought. Almost.

By the time Adam got home, it was too late to call Beth—and besides, what would he say? "In case I didn't make it clear to you before, I'd really like to sleep with you—and even though I am the perfect PC boyfriend and will stand by you no matter what and don't—I swear to you, *don't*—just want you for sex, I think it's natural for me to want that, too, especially since I'm probably the only eighteen-year-old homecoming king virgin this side of the Mississippi"?

Yeah, that would go over really well.

He sounded like one of those Neanderthals in the teen after-school specials they played on local access TV and occasionally showed as a precautionary measure in health class: "But gee, honey, I have these urges . . ."

No, best just to wait it out.

It hadn't always been like this, of course. Back in the beginning, she couldn't get enough of him—they couldn't get enough of each other. He would come over to her house after school and they would try to do homework together, and after a few minutes she would tire of aimlessly flipping through the pages of her history textbook, and he would give up on furiously writing and erasing and rewriting wrong answers to the same trig problem over and over again, and that would be it. He would look up, she would look up, their eyes would meet, and they would be on each other, kissing, stroking, fumbling with buttons and bra straps, desperate to drink each other in, to find every one of their bodies' hidden secrets, to touch, to meld. Sometimes all it took was an accidental touch—sitting across a table from each other, his hand would brush against hers, and it was like a stroke of lightning, a bolt of charge between them, and he would have to have her. And it wasn't just him. There were times . . . that day last spring in the empty hallway when he'd given her a quick peck on the cheek before going off to practice. He'd turned to leave, and she grabbed the back of his shirt collar, pulled him back to her, back into his arms. Then Beth—practical Beth, shy Beth, tentative Beth—had pushed him up against the wall and dug her body into him, sucking on his lips and kneading her fingers into his muscles. Not caring who saw. In the beginning it had been like that.

Not in the *very* beginning, of course. At first they'd done nothing but talk. Which, to be honest, was the exact opposite of what he was used to. They talked and talked— on their first date, they talked through dinner, through dessert, late into the night, until Beth realized her curfew had long since run out and, like Cinderella, she'd fled off into the night. He'd never really *talked* to a girl before (except Harper, and that didn't count), but then he'd never met a girl like Beth, who really listened. Who really seemed to want to know him—not the all-star jock, not the homecoming king, but *him*. On their second date they'd talked

54

even more. About everything—families, school, religion, what they loved, what they wanted. They'd talked, and talked, and that was all. As he walked her to her door, he'd hesitantly taken her hand, and she'd let him. They'd stood in the doorway, her hand warm in his, and he'd slowly lifted his other hand to her face, touched her chin, but before he could lean in, close his eyes, bring his lips to hers, she'd pulled back. Jerked her hand away and slipped inside the house, without a word.

It was on the third date—the date he'd figured would never happen after she'd run away from him on date number two—that he knew. They'd stood in the park, looking up at the stars—Mars and Venus would be spectacularly bright that night, she had told him. And with any other girl, that would just be a tactic, a ruse to get him somewhere dark and alone. But Beth just wanted to show him the stars. They'd stood close together, his arm brushing hers, their necks craned toward the sky.

"It's so beautiful," she'd said in a hushed voice.

"Yes," he'd whispered. But he was looking at her. He put a hand on her waist, another on the back of her head, on her soft, blond hair, and drew her face toward his. And their lips met, their bodies came together. She'd been so hesitant, so scared and tense, almost pulling away. And then she took a deep breath—he could feel her chest rise and fall in his arms—and her arms wrapped around him, her fingers running through his hair and caressing his neck. When they finally broke away from each other, she didn't move away, but stayed close to him, her arms loosely wrapped around his shoulders. At first he'd thought she was crying—but she was laughing.

"I had no idea," she'd told him, when he asked why. "All this time, and I just—I had no idea."

But she wouldn't explain, just kissed him again.

That was the beginning of everything. They had still talked, all the time, for hours, but they talked in quiet voices, their lips inches apart, their bodies wound together. It seemed like it would last forever—but here they were, or rather, here he was, alone.

It was all different now, now that there was this *thing* in their way that they wouldn't, or couldn't, talk about. And that was the problem. It wasn't about what he wanted or what she didn't want—it was about what neither of them could say. She was tense again, scared, hesitant, but this time there was no endless conversation, no soul baring. After all they'd had together, she wasn't turning to him, and he was afraid to push—afraid that this time, if she ran away, she might not come back.

He stripped down to his boxers, fell into bed, and, as his tired mind began to wander, pictured himself back in bed with Beth, curled up tight against her warm body.

Except—

Except that Beth didn't have long black hair that cascaded down her back like a shimmering river, or eyes of deep green that you could lose yourself in for days. Glistening, full red lips and a mischievous smile. And she didn't cling to him, didn't lean on him—didn't need him.

But someone did.

chapter

4

They decided to meet that week to discuss logistics for the party. An anti–Dance Committee committee. Kaia had offered her place—though it was a fifteen-minute drive out of town, on a deserted stretch of broken-down highway, it had plenty of space and came with a guarantee of no parental supervision. And by Grace standards—both Grace the town, whose mining elite had had neither the time nor the inclination to build grand estates even when there was money to do so, and Grace the family, whose four-bedroom house, a holdover from the good ol' days, may have been on the right side of the tracks but was in dire need of a fresh paint job and a new roof—it was a palace. Five bedrooms, three bathrooms, maid's quarters, a shiny stainless steel kitchen that would have been at home on the Food Channel—and the crowning glory, a capacious living room that took up half of the ground floor and was walled by floor-to-ceiling windows that overlooked the wide desert expanse. Kaia's father had flown in an architect and designer from Manhattan, and the two had guaranteed that every detail—from the moldings to the banister of the spiral staircase, from the towels in the pool house to the sterling silver cocktail shaker on the fully stocked bar—worked in concert, creating a pristine world in which everything had its place. (Everything except Kaia, of course, who hadn't been prescreened and carefully selected for her ability to match the wallpaper—and, mainly out of spite, never used a coaster.)

Pool table, hot tub, open bar, an inside glimpse into the lifestyles of the very rich if not so famous? It was an offer even Harper couldn't refuse.

After all the oohing and aahing had ended—quicker than might be expected, since Adam had already seen the place from the outside and he'd had plenty of time to imagine what wonders the inside might hold; Kane's excitement was rarely roused by anything he couldn't smoke, drink, or snort; Harper would rather have died than admit even a fraction of the awe and envy that struck her as she stepped through the doorway, and Miranda loyally followed Harper's lead—they got down to work. Almost.

"So, what's this I hear about a hot tub?" Kane asked, sauntering through the large living room and pausing before one of the oversized windows that looked out over the pool deck.

Harper cleared her throat in exasperation and waved her notebook in the air. "Forget the hot tub, Kane—we've got work to do. Remember?"

Kane spun around to face the room, a slow grin creeping across his face. "Yeah, yeah, work before play," he allowed. "But . . ." He strode to the edge of the room and squeezed himself behind the mahogany bar. "Rum and Cokes before work—don't you think?" He cocked an eyebrow in Kaia's direction—the closest Kane ever got to asking permission.

"Be my guest," she said, shrugging. "That's what it's there for."

"Harper?" Kane asked, brandishing an empty glass at her and temptingly dangling a bottle of rum over its rim.

Harper sighed and tossed her notebook down on one of the leather couches. "Okay. Fill 'er up."

She was only human, after all.

Delighting in his favorite role, Kane began to dole out the drinks—vodka cranberry for Miranda, beer for Adam, dry martini for Kaia, and, of course, rum and Coke for Harper. Finally, Kane poured himself a glass of single-malt scotch, then stepped out from behind the bar and suggested they get started. He was already getting bored.

"So Beth's definitely not coming?" Miranda asked, catching Harper's look and trying not to laugh as her eyes practically rolled out of their sockets.

Adam shook his head. "She's got some meeting for the school paper," he said, frowning. "She told me to say she was sorry she couldn't help out, though."

"Now, how could I begrudge her when she's devoting her time to the worthy cause of Haven High investigative journalism?" Harper asked.

Miranda and Kaia snorted in sync.

"I'm on the paper," Miranda commented. "There was no meeting scheduled for today."

"Some one-on-one thing with her and the new

adviser," Adam explained. "To discuss the 'new direction' or something."

"One-on-one with Jack Powell? Lucky bitch," Miranda sighed. "I guess there's some benefit to being editor in chief after all."

"Hear that, Adam? Looks like you've got some competition," Kane smirked. "And from what I hear, you and James Bond aren't even playing in the same league."

"Whatever," Adam growled. "Can we just get started?"

Harper perched on an ottoman at the end of the room and pulled out a checklist. She loved being in charge, all eyes on her. (And she was studiously ignoring the fact that two pairs of those eyes kept darting glances over to a certain raven-haired beauty at the other end of the room who'd splayed herself out along a black leather couch like a particularly flexible cat.)

But even though Harper was in charge and thus had a power trip to keep her awake, and even though they were planning what Harper was determined would be the best—or at least most entertaining and depraved—after party yet, the meeting was boring. As all meetings inevitably are.

Logistics, list making, blah, blah, blah.

It was hard to keep her mind on topic—and neither the rum and Coke nor Adam's distracting grin were much of a help.

Decisions, decisions.

Miranda would handle music.

Kane—unsurprisingly—volunteered to take care of alcohol and "miscellaneous substances."

Adam, son of the area's most successful—and most absentee—real estate developer, would scout locations.

And Kaia would help, because, "Wow, what a great way to get a better sense of the town!"

Harper thought she might throw up.

Mission eventually accomplished, an afternoon's worth of diversions beckoned.

"What do you say, guys?" Kaia asked, rising from her sprawl and flinging open the glass doors that led out to the deck. "Should I turn on the hot tub?"

Kane, who—bored out of his mind—had been moving at half speed all afternoon, sprang off the couch and tore off his shirt.

"Just show me the way," he said, grinning.

Miranda smiled at the sight of his bare chest, then blushed and quickly darted her head around to make sure no one had noticed. Harper may have been right about Kaia. She might be a "skanky, superficial bitch" (Miranda, for one, felt it was slightly too soon to tell, but she wasn't about to get in the way when Harper went into battle mode), but there was now at least one reason to be thankful for her arrival in town. Actually, plenty of reasons—Kane's six-pack abs, his bulging biceps, his taut back muscles, and the adorable indentation that dipped beneath his waistband. . . . Miranda said a silent prayer of thanks and followed Kane, Kaia, and the rest of the group outside, where a large Jacuzzi was embedded in the hardwood deck.

"My father's midlife crisis has been very expensive for him," Kaia explained, "and very fun for me." She flipped on the jets.

Stripping down to his fitted black boxer-briefs, Kane

eased himself into the steaming water with a satisfied moan, as the rest of his friends looked on in envy and amusement.

"Now *this* is what I call a meeting," Kane murmured to himself, raising his glass and toasting the empty air. He closed his eyes and leaned his head back on the marble lip of the hot tub, taking deep, measured breaths, shutting out the world.

Kaia turned to Harper and Miranda, beckoning them toward the door back into the house. "Girls, I have plenty of bikinis upstairs, if you—oh," she stopped herself, giving Harper a none-too-subtle once-over. "Actually, I guess none of my suits would fit *you*, Harper," she said loudly. "Sorry."

Miranda sucked in her breath. Most guys ranked Harper's delicately curvy body somewhere between Angelina Jolie and Catherine Zeta-Jones (pre- pregnancy and gross marriage to Michael Douglas, of course). But curves were curves—something that the willowy Penelope Cruz clone Kaia distinctly lacked. And *not* in a bad way.

Harper visibly tensed, and Miranda waited, as if watching a wild animal poised before potential prey—would she recoil, or attack?

After a measured pause, Harper did neither.

Instead, she merely smiled gracefully—and pulled off her shirt.

"No problem," she assured Kaia sweetly. "I think I can take care of myself."

And, stripped down to a satin black bra and matching panties (the latest from Victoria's Secret—mail order, of course, since the only underwear within a decent drive of town came from the Wal-Mart off Route 53), Harper strolled slowly across the deck toward the hot tub.

Kane favored her with a long, low whistle.

"Looking good, Grace," he crowed, as she slid into the churning water and took a spot beside him. Even Adam, still fully clothed and pressed against the wall of the deck, flushed a bit and gave her an appreciative smile. Harper shot a triumphant glance at Kaia and then let herself slip deeper into the water, finally submerging herself completely. She burst through the surface, face dripping, hair glistening, and then leaned back against the edge, her slender neck in perfect position to be pummeled by the massage jets, her long, bare legs swung over Kane's lap.

Kaia just shook her head. "Miranda?" she asked. "How about you?"

Miranda looked longingly at the hot tub—and, more to the point, Kane's supine figure stretched out along its width, his head now leaned back, eyes closed once again, arms splayed out along the edge. The Greek god of cocky laziness.

But consider her options:

Borrowing a suit from Kaia—who towered over her by a foot and differed in several other, far more crucial, measurements as well.

Or the Harper approach. Except that Miranda's underwear of choice today was baby blue with yellow polka dots and, in fact, recently purchased from that Wal-Mart off Route 53. As would likely be immediately clear.

Add to this the fact that, much as she was enjoying the chance to examine and memorize every tiny detail of Kane's mostly naked body, there was no way she was going to give him the same opportunity. He was taut perfection; she was, drawing from her always at-the-ready mental list of imperfections, stomach fat and arm flab and thigh cellulite and—well, suffice it to say, she was amply flawed.

"No, thanks," she simply said to Kaia. "I think I'll just sit on the side and gawk at all this partial nudity. Teen depravity, et cetera."

"Yeah, I'm quite the turn-on, aren't I?" Kane called to her, eyes still closed.

"You know I can barely keep myself from tearing off those boxers," Miranda called out sarcastically, pulling off her shoes. If he only knew. She sat on the edge of the hot tub, dangling her bare legs in the steaming water, fighting the urge to lift one leg and begin lightly running her toes up and down his tantalizingly close bare skin. Instead, she flicked a foot sharply in his direction, splashing him with a torrent of hot water. "Somehow I think I'll manage to restrain myself."

Kane opened his eyes, lifted his head, and, steadily holding her gaze, wiped the drops of water off his face. He squinted at her, then shook his head and let it gently drop back down. "Do your best," he warned her in a low voice, "but I'm irresistible—one of these days, Stevens, you're not going to be able to stop yourself from tearing off all those clothes and jumping in."

"Don't hold your breath," Miranda said sharply, hoping that he was right, that someday she'd find the nerve.

But today?

Not gonna happen.

"Hey, how's your meeting going?" Adam pressed himself against the back wall of the deck, the only spot he'd been able to find with good reception. He cupped a hand over the mouthpiece of the cell phone, to prevent the splashing and cackling from the hot tub a few feet away from drowning out his low voice. "Is it over yet?"

"No, we've still got a ways to go," Beth told him. "We're going to be here for a while."

"That sucks." He pictured her in the sparse newspaper office—really a spacious former supply room that Beth had commandeered her sophomore year to serve as the head-quarters of the *Haven Gazette*. Despite the old editions hung proudly on the bulletin board, the short row of out-dated computers lining the wall, and the ever-present stack of reporter's notebooks and old tape recorders available for loan, the room still looked—and smelled—like exactly what it was: a dark, dank basement cave. A flickering over-head light, a fraying couch probably infested by termites, a tiny window that looked out onto a ventilation shaft—Adam couldn't stand to spend more than five minutes there, but Beth loved it. She said it made her feel like a "real" journalist.

"No, it's actually really great," Beth protested, her bright smile so present in her sunny voice that he could almost see it. "Working with Mr. Powell is going to be so much better than last year with Donovan. He actually wants to *listen* to my ideas. In fact, you'll never guess . . ."

Adam sighed good-naturedly as Beth began to chatter about her plans for the paper. He hated how busy she always was, but he loved her earnestness, her passion. The way she threw herself into what she loved.

He grinned—the way she threw herself at him some-times didn't hurt either.

"Anyway, I think we might work through dinner," she finished apologetically.

"What? I thought we were having dinner together," he complained, annoyed as quickly as, a moment ago, he'd been aroused.

"I know, I know, I'm sorry—I was just about to call you and—"

He stole a glance at the hot tub, where Kane was now flailing his arms wildly as Harper and Kaia struggled to knock him off balance and submerge him under the water. Kaia let loose a laughing shriek as Kane grabbed her wet, squirming body and tossed it away from him with a loud splash. Adam shook his head in exasperation. Kane was basically beating them off with a stick, and meanwhile Adam was getting stood up by his own girlfriend. It was more than frustrating, it was humiliating. "Beth, we practically haven't seen each other all week!"

"I know." She lowered her voice into a sexy whisper. "Look, I promise I'll make it up to you. This weekend we'll—oh, wait, hold on."

Adam waited, his annoyance mounting. In the background he could hear distant voices and the familiar melody of Beth's laughter.

Finally: "Sorry, Ad—Mr. Powell needs to go over something with me and the sooner we get through this, the sooner I can get out of here."

Adam made a noncommittal sound. It was better, he knew, to say nothing than to voice the bitter thoughts pounding through his brain.

"So we're okay then?" she asked, sounding worried.

And so he gave in, as always unable to resist the sound of her voice.

"Of course we're okay. Go show him how brilliant you are."

"Thanks!" she chirped. "Talk to you tonight."

"Love you," he told her.

But she'd already hung up.

Adam sighed and stuffed the phone into his backpack. Now what?

He supposed he could go home and sulk, have dinner with his mother—or, more likely, order a pizza with the guilt money his mother had left before leaving on some date with the flavor of the week. Watch TV, wait for a phone call that might never come.

Or . . .

Kane was once again stretched out in the water, letting the jets pummel his upper back and lazily tipping the last few drops of his drink into his mouth. Harper, looking— he had to admit—totally hot, was flicking water on a squealing Miranda.

And Kaia was sporting a barely-there white bikini, which, set off against her perfect tan, made her look like a *Sports Illustrated* swimsuit model. She floated against the side of the Jacuzzi, her chest to the wall and her chin propped up over the edge on her delicate, slender arms. Her hair fanned out behind her, floating atop the water like a cloud of India ink. She was staring right at him.

And that was *definitely* what his mother's trashy romance novels dubbed a "come hither" smile.

Enough was enough. Adam began peeling off his clothes, hoping he wouldn't have to take too much shit for the cartoon hearts that decorated his boxers (last year's Valentine's Day gift from Beth). He could already imagine how good that water was going to feel as he slid in, right between Harper and Kaia.

So, yeah, he'd been stood up—but was he supposed to complain about getting to spend the evening surrounded by beautiful half-naked women?

Maybe the whole thing was, in the end, for the best.

A hot tub, after all, is a terrible thing to waste.

"Sorry about that," Beth said, snapping the phone shut and slipping it back into her bag. She turned back to the table, where a pile of old *Haven Gazette*s lay haphazardly in front of her, all flipped open to the articles she had deemed the best—and worst—of the lot. They were conducting a systematic investigation of everything that was right and wrong about the school paper, and at the rate things were going, it was going to take all night.

"I hope I'm not keeping you from something important," Mr. Powell told her, looking concerned.

He looked so—dashing was the only word for it— when he was concerned. Who knew that there were real-life British people who looked like they came out of a Jane Austen novel? Or, more accurately, a Jude Law–Christian Bale Hollywood remake of a Jane Austen novel. But here he was, sitting only a couple of feet away, poring through the old newspapers along with her, actually *listening* when she talked, actually seeming to care what she had to say. Not that it was easy for her to make much sense, not when she couldn't take her eyes off the curly brown lock of hair that kept slipping over his left eye no matter how many times he impatiently flicked it away. She wanted to reach out and smooth his unruly curls, straighten the silk tie that was loosely knotted at a rakish angle . . . she just wanted to touch him and assure herself that he was real.

"What?" she asked, suddenly realizing that he had asked her something and was, apparently, waiting for a response.

"I said, if you've got somewhere else to be . . . ," he repeated.

"No, don't worry about it," Beth assured him quickly. "*This* is the most important thing right now." She tossed one of the old editions of the paper away from her in disdain. "It's like I've been saying, I really want to make this paper *something*. I want us to publish regularly and investigate stories and challenge people's preconceptions—I want it to be more than just a few pieces of paper that the kids laugh at and then use as a place mat on a monthly basis. And I think that—"

"Whoa, whoa," Powell cut in, laughing. "You're preaching to the choir here. Aren't I ordering us some food so we can get to work and stay at work on this thing? Trust me, you've sold me."

"Sorry," Beth said, blushing. It was easy to get carried away—she'd never had a teacher like Mr. Powell, so young and energetic and—well, she didn't even know that they *made* teachers like Mr. Powell.

"I hope I'm not keeping *you* from something important," she said, suddenly realizing that a guy—man—like that probably had a number of better things to do.

He laughed again and began ticking off Grace's social limitations on his fingers. "Let's see. I'm new in town, don't know anyone, and from what I've been able to tell, tonight's social options range from Wet T-Shirt Night at the local bar to Bingo Night at the local church."

Beth sighed quietly in relief and tried her best not to picture Mr. Powell parading across a makeshift stage wearing only a clingy wet T-shirt and a pair of boxers. Her best was far from good enough.

"I suppose you should be very honored I'm willing to pass it all up for you," he continued. "So, what'll it be? Chinese? Indian? Thai?"

Beth rolled her eyes.

"You *are* new in town," she scoffed. "The only place that delivers around here is Guido's Pizza Shoppe—where the pizza's guaranteed to come in fifteen minutes or 'whenever the hell Guido feels like bringing it.'"

"Sounds like a real customer-friendly operation," he said. "I'll take it. A medium cheese should cover us, I think—do you know the number?"

"Yeah, it's in my phone." Beth pulled it out and made the call. "Thanks again for working with me on this, Mr. Powell," she told him once Guido had answered and, with a surly growl, put her on hold.

"It's just wonderful to have a student who's so engaged," he told her, briefly placing a hand on her shoulder. "I'm here for whatever you need."

Beth flushed with pleasure. "Thanks, Mr. Powell," she mumbled, dipping her head and tucking her hair behind her ears.

"I should be thanking *you*—you're saving me from Wet T-Shirt night, after all." He winked at her, then turned back to their stack of work, all business once again. "Oh, and

Beth?" he asked, after they'd spent a quiet moment sorting through the papers.

"Yes?" she looked up and, despite the temptation to dart her eyes around the room lest he read her expression and the embarrassing thoughts that lay behind it, met his gaze.

"It seems like we're going to be spending a lot of time together this year, working pretty closely and all—so at least when we're out of the classroom, why don't you just call me Jack."

chapter

5

"Remind me again why I ever agree to drive you anywhere?" Adam asked, bemused, as Harper flung herself into the car, still bleary from sleep and clutching a cup of coffee as if it were a life preserver. Two weeks into the school year, and dragging herself out of bed each morning still took every ounce of willpower she had. Some mornings—the ones where she showed up at school two hours late with a forged note about a lingering migraine or unavoidable dentist appointment—it took more.

"Because you love me?" she suggested sweetly, buckling herself in. "Because you can't get enough of me?"

"Because I'm an idiot who keeps forgetting that you're incapable of being on time?"

Harper gave Adam an affectionate slug on the shoulder.

"Just drive, Jeeves," she instructed him. "Or do you want us to be late?"

Adam shifted the car into gear and took off toward the school, while Harper played absentmindedly with the radio. It only got AM stations—but given the overall state of the car, with its clanging exhaust, its nonexistent suspension system, the front doors that would never open, and the back doors that would never quite close, Harper was always pleasantly surprised when the pile of junk managed to make it from point A to point B. A fully functioning radio seemed too much to ask.

Not that she would ever insult Bertha (the car was named after a golden retriever that Adam had been forced to abandon when he and his mother moved here from South Carolina so many years ago)—at least not in front of Adam. He was just a little . . . sensitive when it came to the car, which he had lovingly restored. (It was now only half as much of a piece of shit as it had been, which was saying very little.) But, ugly as the Chevy was, it got her where she needed to go, which was more than she could say for her family's Volvo. Her parents' car never broke down, it had an FM radio and an untarnished paint job—and she wasn't allowed to touch it.

Adam had been giving her rides to school ever since tenth grade, when, courtesy of an early birthday and a generous mother, he'd gotten both a license and a car long before Harper had been able to even imagine a life liberated from parental chauffeuring and bicycles. Now that she didn't get to spend much one-on-one time with him anymore, she'd come to look forward to these rides to a ludicrous degree. (Especially now that she was waging her thus-far-unsuccessful campaign for his affections, a depressing thought she preferred not to dwell on this early in the morning.)

"So, any exciting plans for tonight?" she asked, as they

sped through the streets of Grace and all the sepia-toned hot spots whizzed by—bar, pool hall, gas station, liquor shop, bar. Any quaintness the main drag may have had in the past had leached out over the decades. It was hard to be quaint when all you had to work with was neon, bankruptcy, and decay. "Hot date?"

Adam shook his head ruefully.

"Yeah, hot date with my TV. Beth has another newspaper meeting this afternoon, and tonight she's got some job interview." He sighed and rolled open his window, letting a rush of arid air sweep into the stuffy car. "Dating someone lazier might have been a little less brutal on my social life."

Tell me about it, Harper thought. Once he kicked Little Miss Do-It-All to the curb, Harper (Little Miss Have-It-All?) would be only too happy to remind him of the joys of slacking off.

But all she said aloud was, "I'm sure if she loves you, she'll make time for you." Sweetly. If not sincerely.

Adam had always been the one guy in her life who didn't really appreciate the Harper Grace Bitch on Wheels show—maybe because he was also the only one who saw it for the act it was. Or at least that was his take on things, and she was perfectly happy to keep him in the dark about the "real" Harper Grace. If he wanted to think the hard shell covered a soft center of sugar and spice and everything nice, so much the better.

"Yeah, well, in the meantime, I'm in for the night," he complained.

Harper was about to suggest an alternative, when—

"Or maybe I'll give Kaia a call. She's been wanting to

go take a look at some spots for the party. Could be fun."

Harper gritted her teeth. She'd remained silent on the subject for a week now, saying nothing when Adam invited Kaia to come sit with them at lunch, forcing a smile when he had driven her off on a tour of the "sights," grinning and bearing it every time Kaia accidentally-on-purpose brushed up against him with her fingers, her shoulder, or, increasingly often, her chest. She'd waited for Beth to do her dirty work for her—but Beth was apparently too busy to notice that her carefully trained lapdog was sniffing around someone else's yard, so maybe she'd waited long enough.

"Adam, don't you think Beth might get a little jealous of you taking some other girl out for the night?" she suggested hesitantly.

"Who, Kaia?" he glanced at her briefly in surprise, then turned his eyes back to the road. "It's not like that. Beth knows that—besides, don't you want us to find a place? It's your party, I'd think you would be a little grateful."

So defensive—what was the deal with that?

"It's not that," she protested. "I just don't want you getting too involved with her. I . . ."

Hate her?

Despise her?

Loathe her with every fiber of existence?

" . . . don't trust her."

"You don't even know her!" Adam exploded. "People always do that, and it's not like they know what the hell they're talking about."

"What people? Always do what? What the hell are *you* talking about?"

Adam tightened his lips into a thin and narrow line and, although they were stopped at a light, refused to turn his head and face her. He stared straight ahead, his shoulders tense, his voice hard. "I just—I think you should give someone the benefit of the doubt for once, Harper."

"And what's that supposed to mean?"

"You can be kind of hard on people," he stammered. "And Kaia—I just think Kaia could use a break."

"Oh, please!" Harper burst into harsh laughter. "That girl's entire life has been a break."

"What do you know about it?" he retorted.

"More than you, apparently." She threw up her hands in disgust, then brought one down to rest lightly on his shoulder. "Adam, are you really this naive?"

"Apparently I am," he said stonily, shrugging her off. He turned up the radio, the pounding rock beat drowning out whatever Harper might have said in response.

They drove the rest of the way in very loud, very angry silence.

"I don't know what his problem is," Harper complained. "It's bad enough having to watch him tag along after Beth like a lonely puppy, but if that bitch gets her claws into him . . ."

"Jesus, Harper, dial it down a notch," Miranda said, lighting her friend's cigarette. "Do I have to start making catfight hisses or something?"

"I just can't stand her," Harper growled. She raised the cigarette to her mouth and inhaled deeply, then flopped back onto the freshly cut grass, breathing in the summery smell and enjoying the cool touch of the tiny stalks against her bare neck. She closed her eyes and took a few deep breaths, watching her chest rise and fall, and tried to find somewhere to bury all of her anger toward Kaia, toward Beth, toward everything. When that didn't work, she ripped a few clumps of grass out of the ground, pretending they were strands of Kaia's glossy hair. "This year isn't starting out the way I expected it to," she sighed.

"Yeah, yeah, tell me about it." Miranda let herself fall back onto the grass next to her friend and stared up at the wide expanse of cloudless sky. It was a warm day, not—as was usually the case—blisteringly hot, just warm. If you closed your eyes and held perfectly still, you could almost feel a cool breeze brushing past, the air smelling crisp and clean—a nice change from the traditional Grace bouquet: smog and asphalt. It felt almost like rain, although Miranda knew that the desert rain, if it came at all this year, would arrive as a dirty gray drizzle for a few days in January. Still, there was something sweet and fresh in the air, something that felt almost like fall. Or what she imagined fall might be like. Weather like this should be enough to make you forget everything—the bitchy new girl, the math class they were cutting, the SATs, college applications, and their many, many guy problems.

But maybe that was asking too much of the weather.

"Harper?" she began hesitantly, hoping that her friend wouldn't laugh when she heard why Miranda had coaxed her into spending this period smoking in the football field rather than sitting blankly through a lecture on binomials. "I've got a secret."

Harper shifted onto her side to face Miranda. "Spill it—you know I must know *everything*," she ordered eagerly.

"It's Kane," Miranda told her, avoiding Harper's eyes and instead looking over her shoulder into the distance; she could just barely make out a few small figures scurrying back and forth through the glass corridor that joined the classroom building with the cafeteria and gym. She took a deep breath, forcing herself to continue, trying to convince herself that Harper would understand. "I kind of, I mean, I think I . . ."

Trying to get the words out made her realize how stupid the thought was. What would *he* ever want with *her*? But if you can't tell your best friend your most embarrassing secrets, who can you tell . . . right?

"Well, do you think he might ever want to go out some time?" Miranda finally spit out, all in one breath. "I mean, with me?" she clarified quietly.

Harper sat straight up and peered down at Miranda incredulously.

"*That's* your big secret? You have a crush on Kane? Duh." She flopped back down again. "I thought you had something *interesting* to tell me."

"You knew?" Miranda froze, a cavernous hole opening in the pit of her stomach, her heart beating wildly in her ears.

Harper rolled her eyes in exasperation. "Rand, I'm your best friend," she pointed out. "Plus, and more importantly, I'm not blind. Of course I knew. I've just been waiting for you to break the news." She laughed. "Big secret. Right."

Miranda had to remind herself to breathe. If Harper had figured it out—if it was so obvious . . .

"Uh . . . do you think that—does everyone know?" she asked in a small voice.

Meaning, of course, does *he* know?

"No, no, I'm sure they don't," Harper instantly assured her, realizing she'd sent her friend into total crisis mode. "But what's the big deal, anyway? He's got to know eventually. I mean, are you picturing ramming your tongue down his throat and then taking a time-out to say, 'But don't get me wrong, Kane, I just like you as a friend'?"

"Harper!" A bright red blush spread across Miranda's face—and, judging from the warm tingling she felt from the top of her head to her fingertips and toes—it didn't stop there.

"What?" Harper grinned and stuck her tongue out at Miranda. "You know you want to."

Miranda said nothing, just closed her eyes and began massaging her temples as Harper dissolved into laughter. This could go on all afternoon.

"Okay, okay," Harper choked out through her giggles. "I'll stop, I promise. But seriously, maybe you should just go for it. Tell him."

"Like you've told Adam?" That was sure to shut her up in a hurry.

"Point taken." But Harper was stymied only for a moment. "Okay, Plan B. We—by which I mean I, in my capacity as best friend and master planner—figure out a way to get the two of you together."

"You really think he'd go for me?" Miranda asked dubiously.

"He'd be crazy not to."

"Um, great, but you're my best friend—you have to say that," Miranda pointed out. "Now let's talk real-world possibilities."

"Real world, serious answer, I think it could happen," Harper assured her, without a hint of humor. "And I'm going to make it happen. *Someone's* love life should work out this year, and since mine may be screwed beyond repair, looks like it's your lucky day."

"Can you imagine? Me and Kane." Miranda sighed. She could—and often did—imagine it pretty well.

"Personally, it's not clear to me what you see in the guy," Harper replied. "I mean, I love him and all, but he's kind of an asshole."

"But—"

Harper held up a hand to stop her. "Hey, if it's what you want, it's what I want. I swear to do whatever I can to make him *your* asshole."

"You swear?"

Harper gazed at her solemnly for a moment, then placed her right hand over her heart and held her left hand up in midair, as if swearing in as a courtroom witness.

"Cross my heart and hope to die, may all my hair fall out if I lie," she said in a loud and deep voice, biting the inside of her cheek to keep herself from laughing.

Miranda giggled at the sound of the oath they'd repeated to each other so frequently as kids, when a bad hair day had seemed like the worst punishment the world could dish out.

"Hair swear?" she asked Harper with mock solemnity, extending her right pinkie finger. "Are you sure?"

"Hair swear," Harper repeated, linking her pinkie with Miranda. "You and Kane—it's a done deal."

And they shook on it.

It had become a routine. Every Wednesday, Adam would meet Beth after her English class and they would sneak off to have lunch together, a private picnic in a secluded dusty knoll just off the main quad. They'd discovered it the year before—full of overgrown weeds and bordered by a rusted wire fence on one side and a concrete slab on the other, it wasn't the most romantic spot in the world. But what it lacked in ambience, it more than made up for in convenience and privacy. Some weeks, their Wednesday picnic was really the only time Adam got to see Beth, got her full attention. Other days she might have lunch in the yearbook office, or he would have lunch with the guys on the swim, basketball, or lacrosse team (depending on the season). Then she would have to babysit after school, he would have practice, she had dinner with the folks, he had pizza on the leather recliner while watching *Elimidate*—sometimes it seemed their busy schedules were conspiring to break them up, but Wednesdays? Those were sacred. Untouchable.

They would sprawl atop an old picnic blanket and lay out a spread blessedly devoid of cafeteria food: bread, cheese, fresh fruit. Beth was too nervous to bring any wine or beer onto school grounds, despite the fact that as far as they knew, their private hideaway had never been discovered—but to keep him from whining about the lack of illicit substances, she usually showed up with a Tupperware container filled with homemade brownies or freshly baked banana bread. It was a fine compromise. They would eat, they would talk, they would kiss—and then the bell would ring and they would go back to their crowded and busy lives.

As soon as he arrived outside the classroom, Adam caught sight of Beth amidst the wave of students pouring out. He raised his hand to wave hello, then quickly lowered it again, taking a moment just to watch from a distance as she chatted with her friends, tossing her head back and laughing, her blond hair swinging, her arms whirling through the air as she made some passionate point. Sometimes he still couldn't believe she was all his.

Soon her friends had taken off down the hallway, and Beth stood alone in front of the door, digging through her bag for something and waiting for her boyfriend to show up. As quietly as he could, Adam crept up behind her and gently laid his hands on her waist, whirling her around and into his arms before she'd even realized he was there.

"Hi," she whispered, giving him a soft kiss. "I've been waiting to do that all day."

"I know what you mean," he agreed, and kissed her again, then pulled her into a warm embrace. He breathed in deeply, burying his face in her hair.

It always smelled so good—like lilacs, she'd told him once, but that didn't mean much to him. All he knew was that it smelled sweet and pure—and that it brushed against his face like a fresh summer breeze.

Not that you'd ever catch him saying any of that corny shit out loud, of course.

"You look great today, you know that?" he said instead, stepping back a foot so he could take a good, long look.

Adam had long ago learned that greeting a girl with a kiss and a compliment was a sure ticket for success (you didn't get to be homecoming king by being oblivious). But Beth made it easy. She was a beautiful girl, and today—

unusual for her—she was wearing a light coating of makeup that made her lashes look luxurious and her lips shimmery and moist. And the light blue miniskirt—the incredibly *short* light blue miniskirt—perfectly matched her sparkling eyes. It showed off a few other high-quality attributes, as well.

"*Really* good," Adam repeated, kissing her again.

"Thanks," she said, pleased. She twirled around, modeling the look.

"What's the special occasion?" he asked. "Did your meeting get cancelled? Is our date back on?"

Beth quickly looked away.

"No—no, I still have to go. I just felt like getting a little dressed up today, that's all."

"Good choice," he told her, then was quick to add, "Not that you don't always look beautiful, of course."

"Nice save," she said, laughing. "Flattery will get you everywhere."

She leaned in to give him another kiss, a soft, deep kiss, then nibbled on his lip for a moment and pulled back, giving him a long, appraising look.

"In fact," she continued, her hand tracing its way down the curve of his back and pausing just below the waistband of his jeans, "I wish we could just skip lunch, cut out of here, and I could take you home right now."

It sounded like a good idea to Adam, but he knew better than to suggest it—Beth had never cut a day of school in her life. Even if her hand was continuing its investigations and her other hand had begun twirling its way through his unruly hair, lightly tickling the nape of his neck. It was maddening. Maybe this *was* the right moment to suggest . . .

"Speaking of—you know," he waggled his eyebrows and gave her an exaggeratedly lascivious leer, "turns out my mother's going out of town next week. So I'll have the place all to myself, and I figured . . ."

His arms still around her, he could feel Beth tense up.

"You figured what?" she asked coolly.

"Well, I know you've got issues with, you know, you're always afraid that we're going to get, you know, interrupted—and I thought maybe if we had some alone time, that we could—that you would—"

"That I would what?" she hissed, glancing around at the crowd of students still milling around them. "That I would forget all about my stupid 'issues' and just give you what you want?" She pushed him away.

"Hey, I just thought—"

"I'm sure you did. I'm sure it's all you ever think about—but why don't you think about what *I* want, for once?"

"That's not fair, Beth," Adam protested. How had the conversation gotten away from him so quickly? "I'm *always* thinking about what you want. Why are you getting so uptight about this?" He lowered his voice. "If *that's* all I wanted, it's not like I couldn't find it somewhere else."

Oops.

He knew as soon as the words were out of his mouth that it had been the wrong thing to say. The absolute worst possible choice. But if he hadn't, the blood rising to Beth's face, the thin, angry line her lips made pressed together, and the haste with which she was backing away from him would all have been a pretty decent tip-off.

"If that's how you feel—"

"I'm sorry!" he pleaded hastily. "Come on, please, can we talk about this? Can we just have lunch and talk about this?"

"I'm not hungry anymore. But don't worry, I'm sure you can find *someone else*. Someone less *uptight*." She spit out the words and stalked away.

"I don't want someone else—I want you," Adam said plaintively.

But there was no one left to hear him.

By the end of the day Beth had pretty much calmed down—though every time she thought of Adam, her muscles tensed and her breath quickened, the anger surging through her once again. She couldn't decide—was she angrier at him or at herself? Either way, she was doing her best to keep her mind on something else.

Like, say, Mr. Powell.

Jack.

Okay, so it wasn't a total coincidence that she'd labored for an hour over her hair (silky, straight, and hanging free, with two thin braids pulled around from the front and tied together with a light blue ribbon), experimented with some new makeup, and donned her cutest miniskirt on the day of her one-on-one meeting with the newspaper adviser.

"Deep in thought already?" Mr. Powell asked, stepping into the tiny newspaper office. "Hope I haven't missed any strokes of genius."

Beth laughed and blushed.

"No, Mr. Powell." He gave her a stern look. "I mean, *Jack*, don't worry, the genius is waiting for you."

"Well, then, wait no longer. Your inspiration has arrived! Let's get to work." He sat down next to her and began talking animatedly about his—no, *their*—plans.

They were supposed to be putting together a new layout for the paper, figuring out which fonts and photo borders they wanted to use, where to stick the comic strips and the lunch menus. They were supposed to be debating how large the headlines should be and whether the column "A Day in the Life of a Cheerleader" really belonged in the sports section. *Supposed* to be, but Beth wasn't having too much luck with the whole concentration thing. She sat in front of the computer, an old Mac from the nineties that she had persuaded the school to donate to the floundering newspaper, even though it could barely run the design program they used for the layout. Mr. Powell stood behind her, close enough that she could smell his cologne—something mysterious and European—close enough that she could feel his presence without having to turn around. And then there were the moments when she needed him to look closely at something on the screen, and he would lean down, sometimes placing his hands on her shoulders for balance, and peer over her shoulder, his stubbly cheek only inches from hers. He would stare at the screen, and she, out of the corner of her eye, would stare at his angular profile, wishing the moment would never end.

Beth knew she was being silly, that despite all the joking around, despite the whole first-name-basis thing, despite the fact that last time they had ended up talking together for hours, not just about the newspaper or French class, but about politics, movies, *life*—despite all that, he was a teacher and she was a student. He was an adult—worldly, cosmopolitan, brilliant, handsome—and she was just a kid. Nothing would ever actually *happen*. Of course not. So there was no reason whatsoever to feel guilty about having a little crush—or occasionally wishing that her boyfriend would be a little more like Mr. Powell and a little less like, well, Adam.

Besides, it's not like she was some pathetic twelve-year-old drawing hearts around his name in her notebook or dreaming about how good their names sounded together (although "Beth Powell" did have a nice ring to it . . .).

Okay, so she was being ridiculous. Utterly ridiculous. She should forget about the whole stupid thing, focus on her work, on the newspaper, on her *real* relationship. She should stop wasting so much mental real estate on juvenile fantasies.

But still, she thought, crossing one leg over the other in what she admittedly hoped was a seductive shift in position, she was glad she'd worn the miniskirt today.

After all, it never hurt to look your best. . . .

chapter

6

There must have been something in the air.

Harper stared down at her French quiz, the letters swimming on the page, as she struggled to focus on the *subjonctif* tense instead of on Adam.

She'd been having just a little problem with that all day long.

She'd seen him the night before, shooting hoops in his driveway.

No shirt on.

God, she wanted him.

She had been about to go to sleep when she heard the rhythmic pounding of the ball on the cement pavement—and when she looked out the window, there he was, barely visible in the dim light of the full moon.

Racing back and forth across the driveway, his muscles straining with the effort, his hair wild, his movements fluid, one sculpted pose melting into the next.

So lean and taut, so graceful. His large, warm hands, his supple fingers massaging the ball.

She liked to imagine those fingers grazing her body, climbing through her tangles of hair, stroking her legs. Too bad it was only her imagination; too bad his fingers were, for the moment, taken. Just like the rest of his body, from his thick calf muscles to his tight pecs to the light sprinkling of freckles across his nose.

Her memory was far from photographic, but when it came to the minutiae of Adam's body, in all its curves and spots and ripples, she had total recall.

Harper forced herself to scrawl down a couple of answers and then lay her pen down and closed her eyes for a moment, imagining the warm pressure of his arms wrapped around her, his lips kissing their way down her neck, her shoulder, her breasts. . . .

Her body was tingling, and she raised a hand to her breastbone, lightly grazing her fingers across the bare skin.

If only . . .

If only she would just trust him. If only she would just get over whatever it was that—

No.

Adam shook his head. It's not that sex was all he wanted. He wasn't that kind of guy. (Not that Beth seemed to notice.)

But he was a *guy*, for God's sake. He was eighteen, he loved his girlfriend—was it so wrong that he wanted to be with her?

Did it bother him that all his friends just assumed that

he and Beth were sleeping together? That they would probably laugh him out of the locker room if they knew the truth? That half the cheerleading team would be happy to jump him and tear off his clothes—and yet he was still a virgin?

Okay, yeah, maybe a little.

Enough that he couldn't look at Beth without thinking of sex.

Hell, he couldn't even *think* of Beth without thinking of sex—and sex was the last thing he wanted to be thinking about while sitting in history class staring blankly at his middle-aged teacher and her poorly bleached mustache. But he couldn't stop himself. It was like he was fourteen again—totally out of control.

It wasn't a status thing, it wasn't about his reputation. He loved her, and he *wanted* her—those slim arms wrapped around him, her lithe body tangled up in his, her hair splayed out on his bed. He wanted her—all of her.

And she wanted him, too—he could tell. So what was holding her back?

She didn't trust him. That was obvious. And completely unjustified. He was absolutely, totally devoted to her. And if he thought about other girls sometimes, well, that was normal too, right?

No harm, no foul.

Unless it's just *one* other girl, a small voice in his head pointed out, and Kaia's flawless figure suddenly sprang, unbidden, into his mind.

Now *there* was a girl who knew what she wanted and went for it.

His dream Kaia smiled mischievously.

"I want *you*," she said silently to him, licking her lips and peeling off her damp, clinging shirt.

With horror, Adam realized that he—or at least, his body—wanted her, too. He shifted around in his seat and surreptitiously pulled a notebook onto his lap to cover up, a move he hadn't had to make since the hormonal nightmare that was eighth grade.

And in his mind's eye, the dream Kaia tilted her head back and laughed, chest heaving. And then she went back to the task at hand: stripping off her clothes.

It was just a fantasy, right?

No harm in that.

Just a fantasy, Beth told herself. *No harm in that.* She'd whipped through her quiz in a few minutes and was now left with nothing to do but stare at the front of the classroom, where Jack Powell was relaxing, feet kicked up on the desk and hands clasped behind his head. *What was he thinking about,* she wondered. *Parisian cafes? African safaris?*

When they'd last met, he told her all about his travels around the world, and it set her mind on fire. And his voice—she could listen to those words spilling over her, the impeccably crafted sentences and delicious accent, for hours. For days.

She pictured the two of them sitting across a breakfast table from each other, exchanging sections of the *New York Times* (she'd once seen this in a movie, and it had since seemed to her the epitome of sophisticated romance). Or maybe they'd be working their way through a crossword puzzle together . . . in bed.

Beth blushed furiously, and Mr. Powell looked up, as if he'd somehow sensed that she was picturing what he looked like beneath his chambray shirt and khakis. Their eyes met, and he grinned at her and winked.

God, she loved that smile.

Kane always had a hint of a smile on his face. It was one of the things Miranda loved about him. And that perpetual smirk in his voice—as if all of life was a joke, and only he knew the punch line.

Which, Miranda supposed, was enough to make most people think he was a jerk. And he was. Cocky, pampered, self-centered, lazy, a confirmed believer in "never walk when you can ride" and "never do today what you can put off until tomorrow."

But it was all part of his charm.

She loved watching him in class, the way he leaned back in his chair and propped his feet up on the rim of the seat in front of him, as if he were kicking back in an armchair after a long day's work, rather than suffering through forty-seven minutes of American History. Sometimes he scrawled something on the single piece of paper atop his desk, sometimes he tipped his head back and closed his eyes—occasionally, he even sat up straight and looked at the teacher, though the smoldering disdain never left his eyes. And the cocky smile never left his face.

He was a jerk, all right. A slimy asshole who sailed through life on his good looks, who probably, if asked, would tell you he had never truly cared about anything or anyone but himself. And he would probably be telling the truth—or at least he'd think he was.

But Miranda wasn't fooled. She'd watched Kane for years now. Laughed at his jokes, insulted his attitude, admired his effortless skill at almost everything—noticed the way, every once in a while and only when they weren't looking, he would actually be there for his friends. They didn't see it, they weren't looking for it; but Miranda paid attention. She was an A plus, Phi Beta Kappa student of Kane Studies—and she was convinced that beneath the smirking curl of his lip and the chiseled abs and the perfect tan, there was something else. Something real.

You just had to be willing to look.

Long and hard.

Looking for love was hard work.

There was Ilana: all body, no brains.

Shayna: all brains, no body (but a great sound system—and TiVo).

Julia: all boobs, no ass.

And, of course, Katie: all mouth. Which wasn't necessarily a bad thing. But even that got old.

Sometimes Kane felt like Goldilocks (a tall, good-looking, straight male version of Goldilocks, of course)—nothing he tried out ever quite measured up.

Not that he didn't love the variety—forget too hot, too cold, too tall, too short. It was all a beautiful rainbow of possibility as far as he was concerned, and he had no complaints.

Okay, he had one: He was bored. Even more bored than usual.

Whatever happened to the thrill of the chase, the lust

for victory? That was the problem, actually. Most of these bimbos didn't give chase—just head.

Of course, there was one girl who might present quite the interesting challenge. One girl he'd been waiting a long time to get a taste of.

That blond hair, those blue eyes, all that innocence crying out for a little corruption.

There were, of course, a few stumbling blocks in his path.

His supposed best friend being a not inconsequential one.

Her supposed love for said friend being another.

So it wouldn't be easy. Kane smiled. He was done with easy. Easy was boring.

Difficult? Challenging? Messy and emotional and violent and dirty?

That was more his speed.

That was *fun*.

It's all fun and games until someone gets hurt—and then, Kaia thought with a grin, that's when the *real* fun starts. Now that things with Adam had been set in motion, it was really only a matter of time—which meant it was time to start thinking about what would come next. Adam was, after all, just a diversion. He couldn't be expected to hold her attention for long.

No, she had her sights set on a much bigger fish.

An older, more sophisticated, *British* fish.

She glanced up at the front of the classroom where Jack Powell had stretched himself out in his chair. He looked bored out of his mind.

She knew the feeling.

And she decided that it was time to answer both their prayers.

She knew every girl in the room was thinking the same thing, every girl *wanted* the same thing—she could see it in their hungry eyes, hear it in the way they tittered as he brushed past them on his way to the front of the room. But it didn't matter what they wanted. Because of all of them, Kaia was the only one who had the nerve to act. These pathetic small-town girls could fantasize about him, long for him, *want* him all they liked—but that's all it would ever be. A silly fantasy. As far as Kaia was concerned, fantasizing was a waste of her time—when you saw something you wanted, you took it.

She looked down at the quiz in front of her. Still blank. *Subjonctif?* She snorted. *Give me a break,* she thought. As if she hadn't covered this stuff in tenth grade. This place was so backward.

She grabbed her pen, thought for a moment, and then began to write: large, deliberate letters, the words spanning across the width of the page.

VOULEZ-VOUS COUCHER AVEC MOI?

(*En anglais:* "Would you like to sleep with me?")

A little hackneyed, perhaps, a little cliché—but he'd get the message.

Kaia, after all, didn't believe in being subtle.

She believed in getting the job done.

chapter

7

Harper picked up the phone on the second ring. Thanks to caller ID, she knew it was him and—irrationally—felt the need to smooth down her hair and do a quick mirror check before saying hello. As if he would be able to somehow hear her beauty through the phone. Ridiculous, she knew. But still—every little bit helped.

"Adam, what's up?" she greeted him, lying back on her bed and relishing the sound of his musical voice in her ear.

"Great news—I think I may have found a spot for the party. I just need to drive over and check it out."

It was just what she'd been hoping to hear. She and Miranda had already spent hours burning CDs (no way were either of them risking their personal CD collections on a roomful of drunken teenagers), and Kane had promised them that the drinks, courtesy of his older brother—and a number of mysterious other "connections"—were a done deal. But all the beer and hip-hop in the world wouldn't be enough to make this party work if they didn't find somewhere to hold it, and so far every possibility—the golf course, the gravel pit on the edge of town, some kid's dingy basement—had been a major bust.

Harper knew she should have been somewhat worried, but she had other priorities right now, and one of them—the only one, really—involved getting some quality alone time with Adam. So if he'd found some suitably large, deserted outpost with ample facilities for drinking, dancing, and doing . . . whatever, it seemed only right that in her capacity as leader of this little party squad, she help him with his final investigations. And whatever else he might need help with, of course.

"Cool," she said, as nonchalantly as she could. "Do you want me to—"

"Kaia and I are heading over tomorrow afternoon," he added.

Oh.

She should have known. Since when did Adam go anywhere without Kaia by his side? She shut her eyes tight and tried not to picture the two of them creeping through a deserted building together, hand in hand. She supposed that she should be able to assure herself that Adam was too much of a stand-up guy to ever cheat on his girlfriend— but it was a little late to make that case, given that she'd spent the last couple of months convincing herself that, under the right circumstances and with the right girl (read: Harper), he'd have no trouble doing exactly that.

"So, should we all meet tomorrow night?" Adam continued, after it was clear that Harper wasn't going to be squealing in enthusiasm any time soon. "Hopefully, we'll have some good news."

We. Great.

Harper sighed quietly and sat up in bed, digging her day planner out from beneath a stack of books and papers on her night table. Saturday night was free and clear— plenty of time for sitting around, staring at Adam, or aiming death glares (or at least some finely honed sarcasm) at the girls who kept standing in her way.

"I don't know," she hedged. "I've got this thing . . . but I guess I can move it." Not for the first time, Harper gave thanks that video phone technology had never really caught on. Adam always claimed he could tell when she was lying, something about the way she narrowed her eyes or played with her left earlobe. She didn't really buy it— but still, better safe than sorry.

"Are you sure?" he asked. "I don't want to deprive some lonely guy out there his long-awaited chance to—"

"Shut up," she said irritably. "First of all, this is more important. Second of all, there is no lonely guy—I don't do desperate. Third of all," she added, figuring it couldn't hurt to appear a little in demand, "he can wait."

"If you're sure . . ."

"Positive," she assured him, wondering how it was that she'd become the one talking *him* into this little shindig, given that it was really the last place she wanted to be. "How about eight?" she suggested, trying to muster up some fake enthusiasm.

There was a pause.

"Maybe a little earlier?" he requested. "I have to be out of there by nine—I promised Beth I'd go give her some moral support at the diner. It's her first night of work."

"Beth's working at the diner?" Harper asked incredulously. "*Our* diner?" She smirked, imagining the preppie princess decked out in the Nifty Fifties tack costume (pink tank tops and poofy fluorescent green skirts with crinolines underneath), smeared with ketchup and barbecue sauce and smelling like stale pickles. This day was looking up.

"Yeah, her last job wasn't really paying enough," Adam confided. "You know, her family . . ." his voice trailed off, but he didn't really need to continue. Grace was a small town, and even before Adam and Beth had started dating, Harper had known exactly how that story ended. "Her family . . ." was packed like sardines into a tiny ranch house in a squalid development one step up from the trailer park. Her parents worked three jobs between the two of them and still struggled to buy new clothes every year for their swiftly growing twin sons. Her family's one car, a fifteen-year-old station wagon, broke down more days than it ran. Beth's family, in essence, worked on a simple principle: Ask not what your family can do for you, but what you can do for your family. It seemed that Beth was stepping up to the plate once again—and Harper supposed that she should dig down inside herself and find a little sympathy, or at least a little respect.

On the other hand, there were a lot of things she *should* do. "Should" didn't have much of a hold over her these days. "Could" was, after all, so much richer in possibility.

"So I think it's a great idea!" Harper enthused, as a plan began to form in her mind and a dark smile crept across her face.

"What idea?" Adam asked, confused.

"*Your* idea, genius. Moral support—we'll just have our

meeting at the diner, and then we can all cheer her on. It'll be such a great surprise." As in: *Surprise! Devoted boyfriend that I am, I brought along all my friends to watch you serve and clean and grovel for tips, and basically humiliate yourself in front of everyone you know on your first day of work. Don't you love me, baby?*

Plus, added bonus, Harper realized: a new locale for the meeting would guarantee a nonrepeat of the hot tub incident. Party planning in an empty mansion with plenty of drinks and a giant hot tub had seemed like a good idea at the time—but Harper still shuddered at the memory of the half-naked Kaia rubbing herself all over Adam. *Oh, you look so tense—do you want a massage?* Please, who knew people still used that line? (And why hadn't she thought of it first?) It was a mistake she'd vowed never to make again.

"I don't know," Adam said doubtfully. "She might not want us all there—not on her first day and all."

"Hey, we're her friends, aren't we?" Harper wheedled, twirling the phone cord around her fingers and hoping he would take the bait. "Come on, you're a guy, what do you know about what she wants? Speaking as a girl, I can assure you that she'll be totally grateful."

"You think?"

Eyes narrowed, Harper smiled.

"Trust me."

Late Saturday afternoon, Adam pulled the car into the empty parking lot and the two of them stared up at the dark, abandoned building that loomed before them.

"It's perfect," Kaia breathed.

And it was. The old Cedar Creek Motel (no creek in

sight, of course—only a moldy drainage pipe and a dirty concrete pit that had once served as the "swim at your own not insignificant risk" pool), covered in dust and exuding a stale aura of hollow disrepair. A tilted sign with cracked neon tubing hanging over the entrance hailed the wreck as GRACE'S FINEST LODGING, complete with REAL COLOR TV and 100% REFRIGERATED AIR. The two-story motel, a fifty-room complex on the outskirts of town, had once been painted a proud flamingo pink, standing as a boldly fluo-rescent oasis amidst the desert wasteland; now the grayish husk of a building, sallow weeds nipping at its foundations, effortlessly faded into its environment, an overgrown con-crete cactus. Unlike the empty, gutted storefronts that lit-tered the main streets of Grace, the Creek stood whole and complete—no boarded-up windows, no graffiti covering its walls, no garbage strewn across its empty parking lot. But it had been abandoned for months.

Not surprising—Grace didn't have much of a tourist trade. There was no reason to pull off the interstate and drive twenty miles down a bumpy local road, just to stay in a dilapidated no-tell motel. Tourists had better things to do with their time—and those truckers who did pass through town usually took one look at the Creek and decided they'd be better off sleeping in the cab of their trucks.

Kaia and Adam approached the lobby door—locked, but not boarded up—and Adam pulled out the set of keys he'd snagged from his mother's real estate office. She'd been trying to unload the place for months with, unsurprisingly, no luck.

They stepped inside—and the normal, in color, living, breathing world outside disappeared.

"It's like a ghost town in here," Kaia whispered in wonder. "As if everyone just picked up and left one day, just disappeared—and no one's touched it since."

And it did seem as if the lobby had sat frozen in time since the day the motel's owners had skipped town, a few steps ahead of the bankers trying to collect on a year's worth of missed mortgage payments. A thick layer of dust covered everything, but the furniture, the dingy carpeting, the vintage seventies wallpaper, was all still intact. Preserved. And waiting.

"No one wants to spend the money to clear it out," Adam explained, stepping behind the reception desk and smearing a track through the thick layer of dust with his index finger. Even the reservation book (no newfangled computer system for this motel) still lay open atop the desk, he marveled. He flicked the light switch on the wall behind him—nothing. No electricity, but that wasn't a problem; the afternoon sun filtered in through the lobby's small windows. It was dim and shadowy, but they would be able to see. "They're just waiting for someone to buy it," he explained to Kaia, enjoying, as he often did when he was with her, the unusual sensation of being an expert; she knew so much, but nothing about the West, about life in a small town, about anything that mattered—really, she needed him. And she seemed to know it. "Then the new owners will figure out what to do with all this stuff," he continued, gesturing toward the vinyl chairs and wood-paneled coffee table to their right. "Or maybe they'll just tear it down. Cool, huh?"

"I think it's creepy," Kaia said in a hushed voice, pressing close to him.

Adam had grown up amidst the ruins of Grace's past—playing spies in the empty shells of old factories, hunting for buried treasure around the abandoned mines. But he put a comforting hand on Kaia's back—of course she wouldn't be used to that kind of thing, he reminded himself.

"Come on," he said, leading her through the dark lobby. "Let's take a look. It's perfectly safe."

She stayed by his side, and they crept down the hallway, explorers in a lost world. Not that there was much to explore. The surprisingly spacious lobby, a narrow hall with peeling orange wallpaper and a long stretch of numbered bedroom doors, a cramped staircase leading up to an identical hallway on the second floor (though here the wallpaper was green and purple—or had been, until all the colors faded to gray). And that was about it.

"This is the place," Adam said with confidence, as they surveyed the "courtyard," a paved area by the empty pool with some plastic tables and chaise lounges—he could already picture the scene, drunken seniors spilling outside, dancing in the moonlight, hooking up in the shadows. It was perfect. "It's on the edge of town, so no one will notice us here, it's big, it's dark—this is the place."

"We should check out a room first, before we decide, don't you think?" Kaia asked.

"Aren't you scared?" Adam teased. "Ghosts of truckers past, and all?"

"I think I can handle it," Kaia said with a smile. "Just stay close."

They chose a room on the first floor, at the end of the hall. Adam pulled out his mother's skeleton key and turned it in the lock (Cedar Creek was a bit behind the motel curve—the electric key card craze had passed them by). They stepped inside.

The room was musty and dark, and just as frozen in time as the rest of the building. But it was a motel room nonetheless—bathroom, chair, TV—and queen-size bed.

What more did you need?

"I have to admit," Kaia began, "it looks—aaah! What the hell was that?" She squealed and threw her arms around Adam as a grayish white streak raced across the floor and disappeared into the far wall.

"Did you see that?" she asked between rapid, panicked breaths.

"It's just a mouse," he assured her. "No big deal."

"It practically ran over my foot!" Her arms still around him, she squeezed tighter.

"Hey, it's okay. It's gone now." He rubbed her back for a moment until her chest stopped heaving and her muscles unclenched. "It's okay now," he repeated. She closed her eyes and slumped against him, leaning her head against his chest. He stared at the wall over her shoulder, trying to focus on the complicated pattern of flowered diamonds, on the large spiderweb dangling from the upper right-hand corner of the ceiling, on the critique his swim coach had given him yesterday after a subpar performance in the butterfly heat. On anything but the body quivering in his arms.

Kaia looked up at him, his face only inches from hers.

"Good thing you were here," she said softly. "I'm terrified of mice—but with you here, somehow I feel so safe."

Adam blushed and mumbled something incomprehensible.

"It's funny," Kaia said, leaning closer and tightening her

grip. "I've only known you for a few weeks, but I just feel so close to you. Sometimes I think . . ." Her voice faded away, and then she tipped her face toward him and closed the narrow gap between them, pressing her lips to his.

For a moment he responded, pressing his body to hers, pulling her tight, his lips opening slightly, his tongue gently running along her lower lip, tasting her—

And then he pushed her away.

"What are you doing?" he asked harshly.

A look of surprise and what might have been anger flickered across her face. And then she crumbled.

"I—I'm sorry," she whimpered. "I don't know what I was—you brought me here, and we're all alone, and then you brought me to the bedroom, and—"

"We're scouting locations for a *party*," he yelled, backing away from her. Overreacting. (Had he been sending out some kind of messages? Hadn't he, in fact, kissed her back? But he cut off that line of thinking before it could go any further. He couldn't afford to go any further.)

"I know, I'm sorry—I told you, I don't know what I was thinking. I just—got carried away."

She raised her hands to her face and turned away from him.

"I'm so embarrassed," she said in a muffled voice. "I'm sorry."

Adam instinctively reached out a hand to comfort her, to still her shuddering shoulders, and then, on second thought, let it drop to his side.

"No, I'm sorry," he said stiffly. "Don't be embarrassed. If I—if I gave you some kind of wrong idea, I'm—it's just, you know. Beth. And I—"

"Can we just go?" Kaia asked, turning around again, her eyes dry. "I think we should just go now."

The awkward pause lasted all the way out of the building, across the parking lot, and throughout the interminable ride back into town.

Kaia leaned her cheek against the cool glass of the car window and sighed, remembering when seducing a guy meant slipping into some sexy lingerie, crawling into his bed, and waiting for him to come home and get his surprise. Either that or, if she was feeling lazy, just grabbing the nearest hot guy and pulling him into a lip-lock. No questions asked.

Things were so much simpler on the East Coast.

Okay, so seducing Mr. All America was somewhat more interesting—but it was also turning out to be a lot more work.

She darted her eyes to the left, admiring his profile; he sat rigidly in the driver's seat, hands at ten o'clock and two o'clock on the wheel, eyes resolutely focused on the road. This guy had by-the-book written all over him. Well, that's why she'd picked him, right? She liked a challenge. And even if his heart was still totally committed to Beth, she now had some concrete evidence that his body was less than hopelessly devoted. No, his body seemed to have some ideas of its own.

They hadn't spoken since pulling out of the motel parking lot, and Kaia had plenty of quiet time to plan her next move. She just wasn't sure what it should be. She'd come so close back there, with the ridiculous mouse scare—and damsel in distress had certainly seemed the right way to go. But she was getting a little tired of waiting around for him to sweep her onto his white horse and off into the sunset; maybe it was time to be a little less subtle.

Adam parked the car in the diner lot and hopped out. Kaia waited a moment, and when it became clear that he wasn't planning on opening her door for her (as he usually did), she got out as well. They walked together toward the entrance, Adam careful to keep at least a foot of space between them. Kaia could feel the guilt coming off him in waves, and she made sure to compose her face into the perfect combination of embarrassment, rejection, and vulnerability.

Just to rub it in.

Before they stepped inside the restaurant (undeserving as it was of the name), he pulled her aside, grasping her wrist to get her to stop—then dropping it quickly as if the touch of her skin had burned.

"Listen, Kaia, I'm really sorry—again—if I sent you the wrong signals or something," he stammered, rubbing his temples and looking down at his feet. "I don't want you to feel like, well—" He paused and finally looked up, meeting her eyes. "I'm sorry," he finished lamely.

"Don't worry about it," she assured him. "It's totally okay. I'm okay."

But she averted her eyes and let her voice waver, and she knew he didn't quite believe her.

Good.

"Here they are," Adam said, in a light and brittle voice. He waved frantically toward the silver Camaro pulling into the lot. Harper and Miranda hopped out and jogged toward them, Kane loping behind at a more leisurely pace.

"Well?" Harper asked, before anyone had a chance to say hello. "Did you find a place?"

"Impatient much? Wait until we sit down," Adam told her, visibly relaxing now that it was no longer just the two of them. Kaia suspected that with all the excitement, Adam had almost forgotten their original reason for visiting the motel, or the triumph he'd felt when declaring it the perfect spot. He caught her eye, and the tips of his ears turned a bright red—was he thinking not of the motel's ample party space or conveniently out-of-the-way location, but of the feel of her skin beneath his wandering hands, the touch of her warm breath on his face? She gave him a cryptic half smile—and he quickly looked away.

The group crowded inside and grabbed a booth next to the jukebox. Kaia would have sacrificed a few quarters to save herself from the tedious Ricky Martin song currently booming through the speakers positioned over every table, but she'd taken a quick look at the playlist last time she was there. If you weren't an *NSYNC fan and didn't want to groove to the sweet sounds of Britney Spears or the Beach Boys, there wasn't much there. Kaia grimaced, wondering how much she'd have to pay to get them to turn the music *off*.

As the rest of the "gang" bantered back and forth, Kaia quickly scanned the menu, reconfirming for herself that there wasn't a thing on it she wanted to eat. She certainly wasn't going for the "Sushi Special," the mere thought of which filled her with nausea. (They were five hours from the nearest ocean and no freshwater in sight; the fish on the menu might very well have been, as advertised, the "catch of the day"—but *which* day? And in which year?) She did her best to suppress a sudden pang of homesickness—there was a little place in the West Village that served thirty different kinds of sushi, all better than anything you could get in Japan (which she knew from personal experience). She and her friends had made it a policy to stop there at least once a week—and the secluded park just down the street made the perfect spot for a picnic, as she and an incredibly hot NYU student had discovered one night. He'd satisfied her craving for sushi, and she'd satisfied his for something equally fresh and spicy. One of those perfect New York nights. It all seemed a very long time ago—and very far away.

Thankfully, before she could spiral downward into a cesspool of nostalgia and self-pity, the waitress showed up to take their order—and the shock of it was enough to slam Kaia back into the present. She was surprised enough by the quick service, but she was even more surprised that the waitress, beneath the tacky spangled tank top and gaudy makeup, was Beth.

Beth, her hair pulled up into a high side ponytail and garish blue eye shadow smeared across her lids, looked even more surprised to see them. And not in a good way. She fumbled with the small notebook she used for taking orders and dropped her pen; as she was bending down to pick it up, she came within a few centimeters of smashing her head into the edge of the table. Finally, she stood again and waved a feeble hello, trying to smooth down the wisps of blond hair that had escaped from her ponytail and shifting her weight back and forth from one foot to the other.

"Hey, honey!" Adam said giddily, oblivious to his beloved's disarray. "Look—I brought everyone down to cheer you on. How's the first day going?"

"Yes, tell us, Beth," Harper added. "We're all eager to hear about your adventures in food service."

Beth flushed and shot a nervous glance over her shoulder, where a rotund middle-aged man was giving her the fish eye from behind the counter. Kaia guessed he must be the manager, or perhaps the owner—either way, she shuddered at the thought of his greasy hands coming anywhere near her food. Good thing she hadn't really been planning to eat.

"I—uh, hey guys," Beth said finally, with a weak smile. "Adam, why didn't you *tell* me that everyone was coming?" she added, glaring at her boyfriend.

Kaia could easily pick up on the thinly disguised hostility in her voice. The people across the restaurant probably picked up on the hostility in her voice. But Adam, unfortunately for his peace of mind and fortunately for everyone else's entertainment, did not. (Was he still too shaken from the afternoon's events to participate in normal human interaction? Kaia hated to give herself too much credit . . . but on the other hand, she knew she was pretty damn good.)

"I wanted to surprise you, Beth," Adam said, grinning.

"Well, you definitely did," she acknowledged through a gritted smile.

Before she could say anything else, the greasy manager guy with the bad comb-over strolled by.

"Back to work, Manning," he ordered Beth. "You're on a shift, not a date."

"Yes, Mr. White," Beth said meekly. "I was just about to take their order."

"That's a good little girl," he smarmed, nodding his head sharply.

Beth blinked her eyes furiously for a moment, then whipped out her notebook and drew back her lips in a poor imitation of a smile.

"So, uh, what can I get for you all?" she asked in a coolly professional voice.

"How about the 411 on where I can find an outfit like that for myself?" Kaia asked sarcastically, gesturing to Beth's bright green poodle skirt. "It's just stunning."

Everyone laughed, including—Kaia was pleased to note—Adam. A bit of the frustration of the afternoon slipped away, and Kaia suddenly realized this dinner might be a lot more pleasant than she'd thought. Goodbye damsel in distress, hello other woman.

After they'd downed their drinks and scraped the bottom of their ice-cream sundaes, everyone left—except Adam, who waited dutifully for Beth to finish up her shift. He liked watching her work—she was so efficient, every move measured and practiced, as if she'd been behind the counter for years, rather than hours. As the restaurant emptied out, he followed along behind her as she wiped down the tables and collected the bills from a few final lingering customers, trying to keep her company, but she refused to give him more than one- or two-word responses to his steady stream of chatter.

"Can you just let me finish this up?" she finally said sharply, as he traced his hand down her back. She shrugged him off. "You don't have to wait around for me—just go home if you want."

"No way," Adam protested. "Of course I'm waiting." They'd planned a night out on the town to celebrate her new job—and although the options open at this hour ranged from a stale cup of coffee at the imitation Starbucks to a greasy slice of pizza at Guido's, he was determined to give her a stellar night and make the most of the little time he was finally getting to spend with her. Not to mention, make up for whatever it was she thought he'd done. (And to make up for what he *had* done—though Beth could never find out about that.)

Her shift ended at eleven, and she disappeared into the back to clean up and change. Adam fidgeted as he waited, fiddling with the jukebox, studiously ignoring her manager's glare, and reading the newspaper headlines and vintage movie posters hanging on the wall. *Revenge of the Forty Foot Woman,* read one. *Her love will move mountains . . . and her wrath will crush cities.* Adam shivered—he could relate.

Beth eventually reemerged and, hesitating for a moment, made her way toward the door, gesturing to Adam that he should follow her.

"Hey, you did great!" Adam said, hurrying over and throwing his arms around her. Maybe if he ignored the tension, it would just go away. "How was it?"

Beth extricated herself from his grasp.

"It was fine," she snapped. "No thanks to you."

Here it came. Adam ran a hand through his hair and sighed. "What are you talking about?"

"Let's just get out of here," she muttered, brushing past and stalking out of the restaurant. She walked briskly to the beat-up Chevy, one of the only cars left in the lot, and stood silently, arms crossed, waiting for him to unlock the doors.

"So, where to?" he asked, opening her door for her. She

climbed past him without a word and tossed her backpack into the backseat. "Coffee? Ice cream? Beer? All three?"

"You know what?" she said irritably. "Just take me home."

Adam climbed into the car and slammed the door behind him, feeling an immediate spasm of guilt—after all, it wasn't poor Bertha's fault that Beth was throwing some sort of PMS shit fit. The old car couldn't take too many more fights like this.

"What's your problem?" he asked, hostility seeping into his voice. He put the key into the ignition, but paused before turning the key. Better to finish this. Now. "I'm trying to be nice here," he pointed out. "I thought we were celebrating. And you're being a total—" He stopped himself just in time.

"What? I'm being a total what?"

"Forget it," he said in a softer voice. "Seriously, what's wrong?"

"What's wrong? What's wrong?" she screeched, her voice rising in decibels with every word. "What's wrong is that I was just totally humiliated in front of all of our supposed friends, and you just sat there and watched. No—no, better, you helped!" A few tears leaked out of her eyes, and she angrily wiped them away.

"What are you talking about?" he asked helplessly. "I was trying to be supportive. We all were."

"Yeah, thanks so much for the support," she drawled. "You bring them all here, without asking me, without even telling me—like it's not bad enough it's my first day at a new job, I have to *serve* my *friends*. Did it ever occur to you that might be a little embarrassing for me?"

"Look, I'm sorry, I didn't—you should have said something," he stammered.

"Said something?" she asked, her voice choked with emotion. "When? When you didn't tell me you were bringing them? Or when Kaia was making a fool out of me and they were all laughing at me? When *you* were laughing at me?"

Adam looked down—there was too much pain in her voice, in her eyes.

"Should I have said something when Kaia dumped her milkshake on the floor and I had to get down on my hands and knees and clean up her mess? Adam, how could you not know that would be horrible for me?" she pleaded. "How could you, of all people, not understand that?"

"That's not fair," he protested, holding his hands in front of him as if to stem the torrent of accusations. "First of all, that milkshake thing was an accident—"

"That's all you've got to say?" she asked incredulously. "You're defending *her*? I'm sitting here telling you all this, and I've had the worst night ever, and—and all you can do is tell me I'm being too hard on *Kaia*?" She shrugged and turned away from him. "I guess it's good to know where your loyalties lie," she told him in a muffled voice.

"What are you even talking about? I'm so loyal to you that I—" He cut himself off. Somehow, he didn't think it would help his case to point out the temptation he'd valiantly resisted this afternoon. But his anger rose, throbbing beneath the surface, as he thought about the beautiful girl he'd pushed out of his arms, about everything he had given up, was still giving up, all for Beth. And did he get any credit for that? Any gratitude or understanding? *Anything?*

"You know what?" she asked, when it became clear he was never going to finish his thought. "That's not even the point. I just can't believe you thought this was a good idea. I mean, it's like you don't even know me at all. How is that even possible?"

"If this is the way you're going to be, maybe I don't *want* to know you!" he shouted back, his temper finally snapping.

She burst into tears—but he was far too angry to care.

Harper was tired. Tired of the whole hidden unrequited love thing, tired of being consumed by bitterness and jealousy and paranoia, tired of feeling bested by other girls—blonder girls, bitchier girls, lamer girls, and most of all, tired of sitting around waiting for something to happen.

She wasn't that kind of girl.

Not usually, at least. And not tonight.

So after the meeting in the diner (and Harper had at least derived a measure of pleasure from watching Beth twist in the wind, as Adam cluelessly dug himself into a deeper and deeper hole), Harper had decided she needed a break. A vacation from this unsettling and ineffective good girl version of herself that was trying to forge some kind of honest emotional bond with her oldest friend. A return, if brief, to reality.

Enter Derek.

Derek was blond, built, brainless—and had been chasing after her for months. A few dates with him had been all she needed to deem him more irritating than nails scraping on a blackboard, but tonight? Tonight he had seemed just what she needed.

So here she was, an hour after her unabashed booty call, tangled up in his idiotic arms. It hadn't taken much. She'd washed off the diner grease, slipped into a red camisole and black faux leather skirt, applied a fresh coat of makeup, and been more than ready to go fifteen minutes later when his black SUV pulled up to her house and honked until she emerged from the front door. Derek had, of course, been all over her the moment she stepped into the car—or, as he preferred to speak of it, his "love machine"—but after a few slobbery kisses, she'd suggested they stop off for a drink. If she was going to make it through a night with Derek, sober just wasn't going to cut it. (Though she knew from experience that drunk was an equally unwise way to go; when dealing with Derek "Magic Fingers" Cooper, it was best to keep your wits about you. Moderation, that was key.)

So—one drink. One long drive down a dark road, hip-hop blasting from the speakers, Derek keeping one hand on the wheel and the other massaging the contours of her inner thigh. Harper let her hand creep across into his lap, returning the favor—after all, he was incredibly hot, and with the music blaring, it was too loud for him to say anything dumb that would spoil the pretty picture.

Ten minutes more and they were there. "Lover's Lane"—in this case, a quiet stretch of back road with plenty of cactus tree cover and open space for the picnic blanket Derek "just happened" to have in his trunk. They lay on the scratchy blanket and groped each other, with plenty of heavy petting and heavy breathing. Soon Harper was sprawled out on her back, wearing nothing but a pair of violet satin panties. She was also bored out of her mind.

"You're so hot," Derek said, stroking her breast with his

meaty hand and then leaning in to plant a slobbery kiss on it. "I mean, *really* hot," he added, coming up for air.

"Mmm-hmm," Harper agreed as she shifted position, searching for a comfortable spot on the gravelly, uneven ground. No luck. She shivered—September wasn't such a great time to be out at night with no clothes on, she supposed. On the other hand, she thought, her mind wandering as Derek kissed (or, judging from the feel, licked) a path across her chest, at least the stars were beautiful. She'd never been one for star-gazing, but she needed *something* to do.

"You're hot too," she added mechanically, after it became clear that Derek was waiting for something of the sort. *And was that the Big Dipper?* she wondered idly.

It had been like this for the whole tedious, predictable night. Sure, at first it had been good to be reminded of how desirable she was, but it had gotten old. Fast. Or maybe she was the one getting old—because, for whatever reason, she just couldn't get into things. In the past, she would at least have had a little fun before drifting into boredom. Put her brain to sleep and let her body run on autopilot. But now, it was like she couldn't stop herself from thinking.

And thinking and Derek? Not a match made in heaven.

Not that he wasn't a pretty perfect physical specimen, Harper conceded, running her tongue along the outline of his ear and then kissing her way down his neck. She'd give him that.

No, she wouldn't be lying here naked in an abandoned field on a ratty blanket with some guy who couldn't cut it on the A list. Ripped chest, deep blue eyes, cut biceps, adorable dimples on his face (and butt)—he certainly wasn't getting through life on his wits.

"Did anyone ever tell you that you look just like Lara Croft?" he asked, rolling over on his side and gazing at her with an adoring look that made her cringe.

"Who?" If, in the heat of passion, he was comparing her to some ex-girlfriend, he was even dumber than she'd thought.

"You know, Lara Croft. Tomb Raider." Derek paused in his inch-by-inch examination of her body. "It's kind of lame, not as good as Madden NFL or Grand Theft Auto—but dude, she's hot." He went back to work. The guy was industrious. "Mmm, not as hot as you, babe."

Okay, Harper decided, enough was enough. Seriously—video game chick? Even an ex-girlfriend would have been better than *that*.

Harper abruptly pulled away from Derek and began collecting her rumpled clothes from where they'd fallen during his hasty scramble to strip her bare.

"I'm a little tired, Derek," she said, squeezing into her strapless bra and pulling her top over her head. "Can we head home now?"

"But I told you, I've got protection," he protested, confused. He tugged lamely at her shirt, trying to pull it off again; she wriggled out of his reach. "We were just getting started!"

"Well, now you can get started getting dressed," she informed him, throwing his pants in his face. "Because I promise you this—it's not going to happen."

chapter

8

It had been two days.

Beth and Adam still weren't speaking to each other—
and Beth was desperate.

Which was the only possible explanation for her call. A
last, the very last, resort.

And after all, there was no one else. She hated to admit
it, but after getting together with Adam, she'd drifted away
from most of her girlfriends. There was nowhere else to
turn.

Desperation sucked.

She flipped open her small Winnie the Pooh phone
book to the right page—after all this time, she still didn't
know the number by heart—and began to dial.

"Hey, Harper, it's . . . Beth," she said timidly, once the
other girl had answered the phone. And they began to chat.
Awkwardly pushing through all possible areas of small talk
(big surprise, there weren't too many), Harper at least had
the grace not to ask, "Yeah, but what do you really want?"

though Beth was sure it was at the forefront of her mind. And why not? When had she ever called Harper "just to chat"?

As Harper prattled on about something that had happened to Mr. Greenfield's toupee during third period, Beth asked herself again whether she really wanted to have this conversation. Whether she could actually bring herself to have it out loud. She shuffled through some papers on her desk, began doodling on the back of one, nothing but meaningless scribbles, but it passed the time and calmed her down. Finally, she glanced over at the bed, which she'd neglected to make that morning. The sheets and comforter were tangled and strewn haphazardly across its surface; it seemed a bigger mess than one person could possibly have made on her own, even tossing and turning all night, as she had. It was the bed that convinced her; she didn't want to be on her own there, not forever.

"Harper, can I ask you something?" she interrupted. Harper was *still* talking, laughing about whatever it was she'd just divulged, but she broke off immediately, sensing the tension in Beth's voice.

"Of course."

"Well . . ." Beth had no idea how to begin. "You and I have spent a lot of time together, but we don't really know each other that well, I mean, I guess we're not really *friends*. . . ."

"Don't be ridiculous," Harper said quickly. "Anyone important to Adam is a part of my life. You know how *close* we are."

Beth felt a quick stab of pain at the words—yes, of course she knew how *close* Adam and Harper were. Hadn't she suffered through hours of conversation about how wonderful Harper was? What a great friend she was? How misunderstood she was? Like she needed a reminder that her boyfriend considered some other girl his best friend, maybe his soul mate. (He'd never said it aloud . . . but then, Beth had never had the nerve to ask, not wanting to hear the answer.) Platonic soul mate, she reminded herself—and, after all, why else had she picked up the phone?

"You do know him better than anyone else—probably better than I do," Beth admitted, gritting her teeth. "That's kind of why I wanted to talk to you."

There was a long pause.

"Well," Beth began again, "maybe it's been obvious that Adam and I haven't been getting along all that well lately."

"Really?" Harper's voice oozed concern. "I hadn't noticed—what's wrong?"

"It's been a lot of little things, I guess—but, I mean, there's this one big thing hanging over us. And I think— no, I know, that's the real problem."

"What?"

"You'll laugh."

Of course she would laugh. Harper went out with a different guy every week, and Beth was sure she wasn't pushing any of them away with some half-articulated excuse that she only half believed herself. Not that she wanted to be like Harper. Of course not. She didn't even *like* Harper. But all the more reason not to want the other girl to laugh at her, hold it over her for the rest of the year, spread it around the school that Beth was . . . well, Beth was sure Harper would find an appropriately cutting description.

Maybe this had all been a big mistake.

"I swear, I won't laugh," Harper promised.

"You will," Beth countered.

"Beth, I promise you," Harper said seriously, "you can tell me anything. If you have a problem, I really want to help."

On the other hand, she sounded so sincere—and Beth was so desperate.

"It's sex," Beth said finally. "I've never—well, it would be my first time, and I'm not sure I—"

"You haven't slept together yet?" Harper asked incredulously.

"You probably think that's pathetic, don't you?" Beth held her breath and waited for the inevitable.

"No, no, of course not," Harper said hastily. "You just caught me off guard, that's all. I always assumed . . . but there's nothing wrong with it."

Beth sighed in relief. Maybe she could confide in Harper after all. This thing had been eating away at her for too long, and it would be so good to actually talk to someone about it. Even Harper . . .

"I don't know what's wrong with me," Beth explained. "It's not that I don't want to. I *do*. Or at least, I think I do. But every time we get close, I just freeze up. And he thinks it's because I don't trust him, but it's not that—it's just that . . ."

"You're not ready," Harper prompted.

Beth sighed again.

"I guess so. I mean, I guess I'm not." Why was it so easy for Harper to grasp, but still so hard to make Adam understand? It's not like she'd made some hard-and-fast rule for herself, no sex until college or something. And it's not like she thought there was something wrong with the girls in her class who were doing it—even the ones who were doing it a lot. She had just always thought of herself as someone who would wait. Until she was really in love, until she was old enough—it had all seemed pretty simple and straightforward in the abstract. But now? With Adam? Now she wasn't so sure—what did it mean to be "really" in love? When would she be "old enough"? What did it mean to be "ready"—and would she even know when she was? Would it be when she wasn't scared anymore? When sex didn't seem like such a big deal that might change everything, ruin everything? What if that time never came, and *this* was what it felt like to be ready? After all, when she was with him, part of her always felt ready, more than ready—eager. Hungry for more. It was just that the other part of her, the part that said no, wait, not now, not yet—that part was stronger. And that was the part that stayed with her when she got out of bed. That was the part she had to trust—right?

"So, have you two talked about this?" Harper asked.

"It seems like it's all we ever talk about anymore," Beth admitted. "And he says he understands, but it's like there's always all this tension between us. We're always fighting about something—but it seems like, somehow, it's always about this. I'm just afraid . . ."

"What?"

Beth had never put the fear into words before, although it was always with her, simmering just beneath the surface. Somehow saying it out loud made it just a bit more real, a bit more dangerous. But it had to be said.

"Sometimes I'm afraid that he's going to break up with

me," she said quietly. "Find someone else who's not so—someone who *is* ready."

"Beth," Harper said in a grave voice. "Like you said, I know Adam. He would never do that. He loves you."

"You don't understand, Harper," Beth said plaintively, and suddenly all of the concerns she'd bottled up over the last few weeks came spilling out. "There's something off, and lately it's like, everywhere I turn, he's with Kaia. What if she—and he—I don't know. Maybe I should just—do it, you know? What am I waiting for?"

"You're waiting until you're ready," Harper reminded her.

"But how will I even know when I am?"

"Trust me, when it's time, you'll know," Harper promised.

"And in the meantime?" Beth asked, already knowing the answer.

"In the meantime, you wait," Harper explained. "And if he loves you, he'll wait too. I promise."

"Thanks, Harper." Beth was grateful, but unconvinced. "Listen, don't tell anyone about this, okay? Especially Adam. I'd be so embarrassed and—"

"You don't even have to say it," Harper assured her. "My lips are sealed."

"Miranda, you'll never *believe* what I just found out!" Harper squealed into the phone.

Talk about the light at the end of the tunnel. So the perfect little relationship was missing one thing? Meaning—unless something had happened last year that she didn't know about (unlikely)—Adam, too, was still a virgin. Unbelievable.

She laughed and laughed.

If he loves you, he'll wait, she mused. *Yeah, right.*

Miranda hung up the phone feeling strangely optimistic. Harper seemed convinced that Beth's impenetrable virginity was a sign that the relationship could never last. Miranda wasn't so sure—and as Harper was tossing out the insults, Miranda silently wished that she wouldn't be so quick to forget Miranda's own virginity. But Harper's buoyant tone had swept her beyond all doubt or annoyance. And the feeling of hope was contagious. So contagious, in fact, that when Harper suggested that Miranda call Kane and ask him to the upcoming formal, it actually hadn't sounded like an insane idea.

That was then, this was now. And now her phone was staring her down like a cellular firing squad.

Miranda took a deep breath, gulped down an Altoid (though the minty fresh breath did little for her confidence level), and brought up his number on the phone. She couldn't overthink this, Harper had pointed out. She just needed to suck it up and do it. Whatever happened, at least she would know she tried. Right? At least she'd know she had some balls.

Miranda hit talk and waited, with mounting panic, as the phone rang and rang.

"Hey, Kane, it's Miranda," she said when he finally picked up. She tried to make her voice slightly low and husky, aiming for perky but not too perky, casual but intense, sexy but not sex starved—but most likely, it just came across as lame.

"Oh, hey, what's up?" He sounded vaguely surprised to

hear from her—small wonder, since in all their years of semifriendship she'd never called him (the number was in the phone only as a concrete manifestation of her pathetic wishful thinking).

"So how's your weekend going?" she asked, trying her best to sound nonchalant even as her stomach clenched and her heart thudded rapidly in her ears. She'd always prided herself on her clever banter, but all remnants of wit flew out of her mind now that his voice was on the other end of the line, and the moment of truth—or, potentially, of abject humiliation—crept inescapably closer with every passing second of small talk.

"Better now." She could almost hear the smirk in his voice, and she knew that his deep brown eyes were twinkling beneath an ironically raised eyebrow. She'd memorized his face, and the minute movements it made, well enough that she could close her eyes and see him peering back at her. Which, on a ten-point scale, upped her nervousness level to about a thousand.

Is he flirting with me? she wondered as always—or was this just the only way Kane knew how to talk to people? After all, he also "flirted" with the old woman who ran the cash register in the cafeteria, and occasionally the bald guy with the unnecessary hairnet who ladled out the food from behind the counter. Maybe he just couldn't help himself.

"I'm glad I could bring a little ray of light into your dark and lonely life," she told him, an electric thrill running through her when she scored a laugh.

"So what's up?" he asked, chuckling. "Or did you just miss the sound of my voice?"

"You wish. No, I'm calling because—" Miranda stopped, the words choking in her throat.

Because I want to ask you to the dance.

Because I want to know whether you had a date yet for the dance.

Because I want to come over there and rip off all of your clothes.

"Because, uh, I was wondering if, I mean, do you have—"

"Spit it out, I've got a hot date coming over," he joked. Probably it was a joke.

"Do you have—do you know which chapter we were supposed to read for Setlow's class?" God, she hated herself sometimes. It was an asinine excuse for calling him, which, she supposed, was appropriate, since it had been asinine to call in the first place. She looked down at herself in disgust, at the oversized T-shirt and boxers she'd thrown on after dinner, her lying-around-and-watching-TV outfit. Or, the way things were going, more like her boring, frumpy, destined-to-grow-up-into-an-old-maid-and-die-fat-and-alone outfit. A fate Miranda supposed she deserved, since she apparently didn't have the nerve to do anything about it.

"You called *me* to check up on the homework?" Kane asked incredulously. "Stevens, are you feeling okay? Taken any recreational drugs lately?"

She laughed shakily. At least he'd bought it. She didn't know whether to be angry at herself for chickening out, or grateful that whatever insanity had convinced her he might be interested had subsided before she could make a complete fool of herself.

"Miranda, you still with me?" he asked, when she didn't respond.

"No, yeah, you're right. I don't know what I was thinking. It was stupid. I'd better go," she babbled, all in one ragged breath, and snapped the phone shut before he could say anything else.

Stupid was right.

Adam sat in his empty living room, staring at the darkened screen of the TV. The phone rested on his lap, as it had for the last half hour, ever since he'd flipped off the TV in disgust, midway through some crappy sitcom. He'd picked up the phone, determined to make things right. And then he'd put it down. He'd gone through the pointless routine again and again, even dialed part of the number a few times, but couldn't bring himself to finish.

He wanted to apologize to Beth, of course he did. But he didn't know what to say. He still wasn't quite sure what he was apologizing for, to be honest, or even whether he was the one who should be apologizing in the first place. His mother often claimed that the man was *always* the one who should be apologizing—and that was certainly his father's way. Adam Morgan Sr. had apologized and apologized, but it was, Adam supposed, never enough. At least it hadn't been enough to stop his mother from throwing plates at his father's head, or sneaking a gulp from an ever-present bottle of scotch when she thought her young son wasn't looking. Adam resolved—not for the first time— that there was no way he would ever model his relationship after his parents' short-lived marriage. Better to die alone than go down that path.

Still, Adam reasoned, he'd obviously done something wrong. Hurt Beth in some way. And hurting someone he loved was the last thing he'd ever wanted to do.

He picked up the phone. Dialed the familiar number. Listened to it ring.

"Hello?"

He opened his mouth, closed it again.

Hung up.

chapter

9

Harper had gym first period the next morning. Though this was normally, and with little competition, the bane of her week, she was actually looking forward to it this time—it would give her just the opportunity she needed. Kane was stuck in gym too—killing time on the basketball courts while the girls paraded lazily around the tiny track. The geniuses behind Haven High's physical education program had a somewhat lackadaisical attitude when it came to female participation. The guys had a rigidly determined schedule: football one week, soccer the next, running sprints the week after that. If the girls, on the other hand, chose to opt out of the period—or because of their periods—and do some "power walking" around the track instead, that was fine.

Harper knew it was sexist and offensive and she should probably lead a schoolwide campaign to remedy the problem . . . but since she hated gym even more than she loved muckraking, she had little incentive to do so. Besides, sexism sometimes came in handy—this morning, for instance.

As she stood in the middle of the ragged field with the rest of the girls, waiting for the teacher to explain the morning's paltry athletic task, she figured she'd soon have no problem sneaking off, grabbing Kane, and doing Miranda's dirty work for her.

It was no surprise that Miranda had chickened out the night before. The only surprise was that Miranda had even entertained the idea of asking Kane out in the first place. Harper had only suggested it as a joke, an empty dare. She'd never expected Miranda to actually buy into the idea.

Small wonder that she hadn't followed through.

"Kane," Harper called to him, once she'd made it safely over to the courts. She poked her face through the chain-link fence and waggled her fingers at him. "Over here! I need you for a minute."

Kane tossed in an effortless layup that swished through the net and jogged over to join her.

"What's up, lover?" he asked, his familiar smirk already painted across his face. (Kane's motto: Never leave home without it.) Only Kane could still look debonair in a Haven High gym uniform—bright orange T-shirt and ungainly brown shorts. Harper wasn't too thrilled to be seen out in public in the female version, especially by the entire guys' gym class, but sometimes you had to make sacrifices for your best friend. Plus, the T-shirt was a couple of sizes too small and she knew that despite the hideous color, it showed off more than a few of her best attributes. Kane, for one, blatantly sizing her up, didn't seem to mind.

"Who are you taking to the stupid dance next week?" she asked, skipping the small talk.

"Ah, I don't know if I'm even going," he told her, shrugging. "I'm sick of the girls here—great asses but no spines." He paused for a moment, then widened his eyes in a purposely exaggerated look of surprise. "Why, Grace, was that just your clumsy way of asking me out? I'm flattered, I'm flabbergasted, I'm—"

"An idiot, I know," she cut in. "Now shut up." She took a quick look around, making sure no one could overhear them. While a few of Kane's cronies had stopped shooting hoops and were clustered together on the court looking over at the two of them, they were safely out of earshot. "Look, I think you should ask Miranda."

Kane burst into laughter.

"And why the hell would I do that?"

Harper smacked him on the shoulder.

"What's wrong with you?" she asked irritably. "Why wouldn't you do that?"

"Harper, it's *Miranda*," he protested.

She stared blankly at him.

"I mean, she's great and all—smart, fun—"

"Beautiful, witty, a great dancer," Harper continued.

"Yeah, whatever—but it's still Miranda." He rolled his eyes, but Harper just looked at him, her face betraying no expression. "As in 'Miranda, can I copy your math homework?'" he continued. "Or 'Miranda, what's a seven-letter word for sarcastic?', not 'Miranda, how I love to lick whipped cream off your breasts.'"

Harper took a quick step back.

"Please, please tell me you've never actually said those words to a girl," she begged him.

"*Woman*, actually," he bragged.

"God, you're pathetic. And now that image is burned into my brain. Thanks."

He just smiled at her, the picture of innocence.

"So you can see why I'm not going to ask her, right, Grace?" He paused, and then a glimmer of understanding dawned on his face. "Why'd you ask, anyway—does she have a little crush on me or something?"

He started to laugh again, but she cut him off quickly.

"As if she'd go for an idiot like you—no, I was trying to do *you* a favor," Harper said, thinking fast. "I figured you've probably had your fill of bimbos by now. Obviously, I was wrong." And she began to walk away. Even pretending to jog around a track would be better than this.

"Harper, wait!" he called after her. "I've actually been meaning to talk to you on exactly that topic," he said conspiratorially once she'd turned back around.

"Bimbos?" she asked, raising an eyebrow.

"Being fed up with them. I've got my eye on someone new, and I think you're just the girl to help me get her."

"The great Kane Geary—actually admitting he needs someone's help?" Harper was still disgusted—but also intrigued. "And who is this unapproachable goddess?"

"Beth." Kane had the grace to look at least slightly abashed.

"Oh, Jesus Christ," Harper swore. What was it about the Bland One that made her so irresistible? "Why would I want to help you with that?" she asked in a more measured voice. "Adam's one of my best friends—and, incidentally, I thought he was one of yours, too. I'm supposed to help you steal his girlfriend?"

Now it was Kane's turn to raise an eyebrow.

"Come on, Harper, I think we both know why you'd have an interest in breaking up Ken and Barbie—do you really need me to say it out loud?"

Harper feigned ignorance, said nothing.

"I've seen the way you look at him, Grace. I know you want this as much as I do—and there's no one else I'd rather have on my side. Who's more devious than you?"

"Flattering as that is . . ." Harper murmured, her mind spinning through options at a furious speed. Kane and Beth . . . It was true that there was only one person at Haven High more devious than Harper: Kane himself. If he'd targeted Beth as his next conquest—and if the two of them worked together . . .

And then she remembered Miranda. And the promise she'd made.

"Sorry, Kane." And she was—more than she could allow herself to let on. "Much as I'd like to take part in your sordid little plot, I think I'll sit this one out. I do have a *few* principles, you know."

Kane looked skeptical. Even more so than usual.

"Doesn't sound like the Harper I know." He shrugged. "Well, I'll still be here when you change your mind. And trust me, Grace: You will."

"He said he doesn't really see you that way."

The words were still echoing through Miranda's mind. She pressed herself against the locked door of the bath-room stall, trying to slow her panicky breathing.

Harper seemed to think there was still hope, that Kane just needed to see the light—that he thought Miranda was smart, beautiful, funny, etc.

Whatever.

Miranda knew the truth and—she should just admit it to herself—she'd known it all along. Kane could never be interested in someone like her. She was too pale, too bland, too ugly—too everything. And, on the other hand, just not enough.

Harper Grace's loyal sidekick. Everyone's best pal. Good for a joke—and not much else.

Miranda had nodded calmly when Harper sat her down at lunch and gave her the bad news, then said, with a wry smile, "Well, his loss, right?"

That was her thing, after all. Living on the surface, never taking things too hard, never letting bad news knock her off stride, the voice of reason and moderation to Harper's nonstop drama. Always neurotic, but always staying just a few feet back from the edge. Harper was the one who lived life on the brink. Miranda just watched.

She'd lasted ten minutes. One minute of deliberate deep breathing as Harper told her the bad news, and one minute of concerted effort to keep her face perfectly still and the tears from falling as Harper tried to console her. Two minutes of laughing it off, to convince Harper that consolation was uncalled for. Five minutes of forced gaiety when a group of girls sat down with them and began gossiping about homework and music videos and what they were planning to wear to the dance next week. And one minute of torture, as she pushed the food back and forth on her tray, blood thumping in her ears loudly enough to drown out the chatter swirling around her, the claustrophobic panic boiling within her threatening to burst out. Almost one minute too many, and that's when she'd left—just in time.

She'd pushed herself back from the table, walked slowly out of the cafeteria, and raced down the hallway to the nearest girls' bathroom. It was only after she'd brushed past the two skater punks smoking by the sinks and slammed herself inside one of the stalls that she'd allowed herself to burst into silent tears.

Chest heaving, she berated herself for getting her hopes up, for thinking she had a chance. Not with a guy like that.

Lester Lawrence, captain of the chess team, who'd sent her one love letter, written in iambic pentameter, every week for a year? Vince Weiss, who'd taken her to the Starview Theater's annual showing of *It's a Wonderful Life*, spent the first hour trying to devour her with his large, saliva-covered lips and the second hour trying, unsuccessfully, to pick his gum out of her hair?

That was her league. That was her life.

Miranda felt her stomach churning and regretted the two brownies she'd scarfed down in the cafeteria, a chocolate chaser for the fries and meat loaf. Harper always lost her appetite when she was nervous or upset, but Miranda had no such luck. No crisis was too small, no emotional tailspin too shallow that Miranda's appetite didn't decide her woes deserved a piece of cake.

Because when you're truly upset, she thought bitterly, *turning yourself into a fat, ugly blob is just what you need to make yourself feel better.*

She sagged against the cool wall of the stall and noticed, among the graffiti advising "Lacey" to "suck this" and suggesting that all guys were either "dicks," "pigs," or, in a nice display of creativity, "bottom-dwelling, scum-sucking creatures of darkness," a new warning etched into the plastic: "Remember, girls: This is a no purging zone! :)"

Skinny, sanctimonious bitch, Miranda thought.

It was the smiley face that really got her—she could imagine the girl's perky voice warning of the evils of eating disorders and the benefits of a healthy diet. As if she, whoever she was, knew anything about—well, anything.

With a grim smile, Miranda pulled out her thickest black pen and scribbled over the "no" in "no purging zone."

Then she leaned over the toilet, stuck her finger down her throat, and made it official.

chapter

10

The words were completely innocent: "Kaia, can I see you after class for a moment, please?"

But the tone told Kaia all she needed to know—specifically, that Jack Powell had finally gotten around to grading those pop quizzes. And had thus finally discovered her little invitation. Took him long enough.

She stayed in her seat as the rest of the class filtered out of the room, alleviating her boredom and excising some nervous energy by mentally rating the girls who filed past her. Too fat, too short, too thin, too gawky, too geeky—no, not too much competition at all, Kaia decided. There was Harper, of course, undeniably gorgeous, if in a seedy, film noir kind of way; but from what Kaia had observed, Harper had too many other things on her mind to think about screwing their French teacher. Her forbidden fruit grew on a different tree. Still, the sultry brunette shot her a curious look as she stepped out of the room. Probably wondering whether to be pleased that Kaia was—to all outward appearances—getting into some kind of trouble, or dismayed because she had snagged some one-on-one face time with Haven High's Most Wanted.

When the room had emptied out, Kaia finally stood and walked slowly to the front of the room, where Jack Powell maintained his customary position, arms crossed behind his head and legs propped up on the desktop. A perpetual five o'clock shadow only added to his good looks; it gave a much-needed edge to his boyish charm. And Kaia was all about edge.

"What can I do for you, Mr. Powell?" she asked, sitting down across from him and watching his eyes follow her leg line up from her low heels to the high slit in her snug-fitting skirt. It was always nice to be appreciated. "Or should I just take this as a yes?"

Powell looked taken aback, then leaned forward in his chair and grinned.

"Well, you're bold, I'll give you that," he told her. He pulled out a piece of paper from the top drawer of his desk—Kaia recognized her telltale scrawl across the page.

"I'm sure you can guess why I've asked you here, Kaia," he began.

Oh, she could guess all right—although the classroom was a bit public for her tastes.

"Well, I didn't think it was to work on my pronunciation skills."

Powell laughed. "No, you've demonstrated quite a— proficiency in the subject matter," he admitted. "I want to talk to you about what you wrote here," he said, tapping the page with his index finger. "I'm flattered, Kaia, I really am."

"As you should be." She smiled to let him know she was joking. Sort of.

"But this sort of thing, teacher-student—it can't happen."

She leaned in, giving him easy visual access down the dark crevasse of her cleavage, if he wanted it—which, she could tell, he did.

"Oh, it *can* happen, Mr. Powell," she assured him. "Trust me, I've seen it."

"Okay, then," he said, folding the quiz in half and methodically tearing it into small pieces, letting them filter through his fingers and drift down into the trash can. "It *won't* happen. Don't be embarrassed," he added quickly. "It's very common that a student develops a crush on a teacher, especially since you're new here. I'm sure it's been a little tough for you to adjust. I can empathize."

"Mr. Powell," she interrupted him coolly, "I think you've got the wrong idea. This is not some sweet schoolgirl crush. I'm not in love with you, nor do I dream of marrying you someday and bearing your British schoolteacher children."

"I didn't say—"

"What I'm offering you is a simple physical relationship with a very attractive woman," she informed him. "So if we're going to talk about this, let's do it adult to adult, instead of pretending I'm some kind of blushing virginal teenybopper. Because I'm not."

"That much is obvious." His voice hardened, the genial warmth replaced by a sliver of ice. "You want to be treated as an adult?" he asked, offering a condescending smile. "I make it a policy not to get involved with my students—but even if that were not the case, I wouldn't touch you, Ms.

Sellers. Not if you paid me. You're trouble dressed up in a miniskirt, and I'd have to be blind not to see it."

She tried to interrupt, but he cut her off.

"Blind and stupid—which must be what you think of me if you imagined this little Lolita act was actually going to work."

"Mr. Powell, I—" Kaia broke off in midsentence. For once, she was speechless.

He sat up straight and smiled at her, but the smile never touched his eyes.

"Play all the games you want with the boys your own age, Kaia, and have fun." He folded his arms on the desk and leaned toward her, their faces now separated by only a few inches of frosty air. "But trust me—I'm way out of your league."

Kaia left the classroom fuming . . . but intrigued. This new and improved Jack Powell was even sexier than the old one. Who didn't prefer Colin Farrell to Colin Firth? No, this cold, calculating front was definitely hot. And promising.

After all, any teacher willing to speak to a student like that clearly had a somewhat flexible understanding of standard school policy—whatever he may have said, she knew he'd be up for bending the rules. It was just a matter of getting him to bend in the right way.

But she still needed something to keep her entertained in the meantime. Down but not out, she decided to take Mr. Powell's advice and pick on a boy her own size.

So, onward to the boys' locker room. (Where else?)

By her calculations, the swim team should be just about

finished with their practice—which meant that Adam, who despite his halfhearted commitment to the sport was too much of a stand-up guy to ever skip a practice—should be on his way in. Hot, wet, and mostly naked. Perfect.

She burst through the door, and the locker room echoed with enraged shouts as flustered jocks as they whipped towels around themselves and ran from Kaia's prying eyes.

"Get out of here!"

"What gives!"

"Hey, baby, you want some of this?"

"Trust me, boys, I've seen it all before," she said calmly as they shouted her down. And while that was true, it didn't mean that she couldn't appreciate a repeat performance. Once again, she marveled at the caliber of male bodies this tiny town had produced.

She threaded her way through the crowd of flesh, searching for Adam, finally spotting him on the edge of the sea of muscles.

Those orange bikini briefs didn't leave much to the imagination.

"What the hell are you doing here, Kaia?" he asked, when she stopped just in front of him and stared him down. "Is something wrong?"

"Nothing's wrong," she said sweetly. "I just wanted to see you." *All* of you, she could have added—but it seemed redundant.

"It couldn't have waited?" he asked, wrapping a towel around himself protectively and slowly inching away from her.

"I'm tired of waiting," she explained, taking his hand

and threading her fingers through his. He pulled away and shot a quick look behind her, where the rest of the guys on the swim team were toweling off and throwing clothes onto their wet and sticky bodies as quickly as possible. Each was keeping a close eye on the live-action soap opera.

"What are you talking about?" he hissed, dropping the towel and pulling on a pair of jeans over his sopping briefs. He grabbed the rest of his clothes and ushered her over to a—relatively—more private area behind a bank of lockers. "Tired of waiting for what?"

"For this," she said, and grabbed his face and kissed him, sucking in the taste of his soft lower lip before he harshly shoved her away.

"Kaia, what the fuck . . . ?"

"What? You didn't enjoy that? You didn't *want* that?" she challenged him.

"Can you please lower your voice?" he whispered frantically. He peered around the edge of the locker—the room had pretty much emptied out, but a few swimmers still lingered, hoping for some excitement.

"Can you get out of here, guys?" he called out. "Come on, help me out here!"

He turned back to Kaia.

"What are you trying to do to me?" he asked in a low and urgent voice. He suddenly looked down and, realizing his chest was still bare, quickly pulled on a T-shirt, the thin white cotton clinging to his wet body. "It's going to get back to Beth that you came looking for me here. She'll freak."

"To be honest, Adam, I don't really care," Kaia

explained patiently. "And I'm not sure why you do, either."

"Kaia, I'm *in love* with her," he shouted in frustration. "You know that. You said you understood. That the whole thing, that other thing, was a mistake, that—"

"Forget what I said," she cut in. Now she knew she'd done the right thing, shucking the good girl act and coming after him hard and fast. Being soft and subtle, giving him time to think and regret before he acted, would never have worked. She needed him to stop thinking and start *acting*. And for that, he needed to know exactly what was on the table—exactly what he would be passing up.

"It wasn't a mistake," she informed him. "When we were in that motel, I wanted you. Just like I want you now." She placed a hand on the waistband of his jeans, then let it slide slowly downward. "And you can't tell me you don't want me, too."

He shoved her away. Hard. She slammed into the lockers behind her with a crash. The shock of impact was mirrored on his face when he saw how hard he'd pushed her. But he shook it off, letting anger sweep over him again— and she was glad of it. Finally, some real, deep emotion breaking through that placid surface. Some passion. Kaia knew what that meant—it was only a matter of time. She couldn't suppress the smile.

He saw the look on her face and shook his head violently, backing away.

"Forget it, Kaia," he snapped, stuffing his belongings into his backpack as quickly as he could. "It doesn't matter what you want, or what you think I want. It can't happen. It *won't* happen."

It was the second time in an hour that Kaia had heard

those words. This was getting old—but once again, Kaia was certain: He may have *said* no. But he *meant* soon.

Adam slammed through the door of the locker room, with Kaia close behind him. This whole situation was maddening. Okay—flattering, too, but also completely out of control. *Kaia* was out of control. And word was sure to get back to Beth and —

Uh-oh.

Looks like word wouldn't have to.

Beth was standing in the hall outside the locker room, facing the door, so Adam got a good look at her face as he walked out—the tentative smile when she saw him, twisted into a grimace of disgust a moment later as Kaia emerged, the front of her shirt still soaking wet from when she'd pressed herself up against Adam's bare and dripping chest.

"See you later, Adam!" Kaia said pleasantly, as the couple stared at each other in silence. She smiled sweetly at Beth, then turned back to him. "Thanks *so* much for your help in there." And she strode away down the hall.

Adam stopped in the doorway, as if half considering a retreat back into the locker room. Maybe if he went inside, came out again, the world would give him a do-over, and he and Beth could start afresh.

Unfortunately, Beth didn't look like she was much in the mood for fresh starts. She stood a few feet away, pressed against the brick wall as if she needed it for support. Her hands were clasped in front of her, in a loose and relaxed pose betrayed by the tension in her frozen face. She wore a light gray, short-sleeved sweater that he'd never seen before. It was the soft color of mist, the same gray that flecked her clear blue eyes. Her eyes, he noticed, were glassy, unshed tears pooling at the lids. She looked very angry—and very beautiful.

"Beth," he finally said. "Uh, what are you doing here?"

"I came to find you," she said mechanically, staring off in the direction Kaia had gone. "I was going to apologize. One of the guys told me you were still in there. So I waited."

Thanks a lot, guys, Adam thought. That was some team loyalty for you.

"I'm glad you did," he said hesitantly, taking a step toward her and gently grasping her hand. "I wanted to talk to you, too."

The contact seemed to shake her out of her state of shock—she whipped her hand away.

"I said I *was* going to apologize," she corrected him. "Past tense. That was before I . . . interrupted you." She looked away. "I guess you weren't expecting to see me here."

"What's that supposed to mean?"

"You know what it means." She swiped a hand quickly across her eyes and finally met his gaze. Her lower lip was trembling—and she looked at him as if he were a mysteriously familiar stranger, someone she'd once known, long ago. "God, Adam, in public? In the locker room? What were you thinking? Did you think I wouldn't find out?"

"You don't even know what you're talking about!" he protested. The best defense, after all, was a good offense. Not that he had anything to be defensive about. He hadn't *done* anything—was it his fault that Kaia kept chasing after him? Wasn't the point that he kept turning her away?

Didn't that, in fact, make him a *better* boyfriend? What more did she want from him?

"What do you think happened in there?" he snapped, losing his patience. "You think I threw her down and *did* her? Right there on the floor in front of half the swim team? Do you even want to know what really happened? Maybe you'd rather just assume the worst." He heard the words coming out as if someone else had spoken them— surely it hadn't been him. Surely he wouldn't say something so hurtful to someone he loved. Surely he wasn't that kind of guy.

"What's the point in asking if you're just going to lie to me?" Beth asked, furiously blinking back tears. "I see the way you look at her—I know you think she can give you what you want. Fine—go get it." She whirled around, as if to leave, but he grabbed her arm and tugged her back around. She wasn't walking away, not this time. All of this, the constant fights over nothing, the tears, the silent treatment, it had to end. They had to actually deal with this—which meant she was, for once, going to have to stick around.

"I'm so sick of you making everything about sex," he spit out, totally exasperated. How many times could they have the same conversation?

"Me? What about you? You—"

"No, *you*," he argued. "This is not about sex, or Kaia, and you know it." And he tried to force the image of her clinging to his wet body, of her lips on his, of her arms wrapped around him, out of his head. "This is about *you*. About you not trusting me. Not trusting us."

Beth's face softened, and for a moment Adam thought he'd gotten through to her. Then she shook her head.

"No. No!" She flung his arm off and pushed him away. "You can't turn this around on me—this is about *you* acting like a jerk. This is about *you* skulking around in a boys' locker room with another girl. This is about *you* wanting—" Her voice broke. "Wanting what you can't have and acting like it's all my fault."

"Beth . . ."

"Of course I don't trust us," she said dully, sounding suddenly exhausted. "Right now, us sucks."

She walked away—and this time, he let her go.

"Thanks for the heartfelt apology!" he called after her, punching the wall in frustration. The stinging pain in his knuckles only made him angrier.

This was his reward for doing the right thing? For resisting temptation? He might as well have thrown Kaia down on the locker room floor, torn her clothes off, satisfied his every pornographic desire—why the hell not, if that's what Beth was going to believe either way?

He'd been there for her, he'd thrown himself into this relationship, he'd done everything he could for her—and she couldn't even be bothered to ask him for the truth. She couldn't be bothered to stick around for a damn conversation.

And you know what?

Good riddance.

chapter

11

She'd never known a knee could be so sexy.

But there it was. Under the table. An inch away.

She could feel his leg there next to hers, could imagine moving hers over just a bit, just an inch, pressing their legs together. And that's not all she could imagine. He was so close—she could just slip her foot out of her shoe, slide her toes up his calf, trace a gentle design across his skin. She could reach out, take his hand in hers beneath the table, massage his fingertips and then press him against her body, so hungry for his touch. . . .

"Harper? What are you thinking about?"

Adam's warm voice startled her out of her frozen reverie. And thank God for small favors—if she didn't stop obsessing over her stupid fantasies, she might miss the chance to turn them into reality. And that's what this was—her chance.

"Harper?" he repeated, sounding concerned. "What's up?"

"Nothing—don't worry about it," she assured him.

"Are you sure?"

"No, I'm fine, it's nothing," she said again. "Besides, I'm supposed to be cheering *you* up. What are you thinking about? As if I have to ask . . ." Beth, of course. It was always Beth. Whether they were in the gazing-into-each-other's-eyes-there's-only-two-of-us-in-the-whole-world mode, or in the I-may-never-speak-to-you-again mode (as, happily, they were tonight), Harper knew that the Blond One was never far from his thoughts.

But Adam just laughed. "No, I'm not thinking about her, Harper, I swear—I'm just enjoying the music. Thanks again for dragging me out tonight."

It had been a brilliant idea—after all, who knew how long Beth would be stupid enough to stay away sulking, leaving Adam on the open market? Opportunities like this didn't come along very often and didn't last for very long—so Harper was planning to take full advantage of this one while she had it. Seize the day, right? She looked around at the grungy bar, the local band that was—just barely—cranking out something that bore a distant relation to music, and sighed. If only she didn't have to seize the day in such seedy surroundings. Though she had to admit, what with the darkness, the haze of smoke, the music (sort of), the place had possibilities. . . .

Of course, a *true* friend probably wouldn't take advantage of Adam's postfight instability, wouldn't do her best to talk him out of a relationship he clearly wanted to stay in (not that she planned to stick with talking)—on the other hand, Harper reminded herself, wasn't it her duty as a true friend to help him see the error of his ways?

"You know I'm always here for you, Adam," she said,

hoping he would hear the emotion in her voice, would, for once, realize what all her loyalty, all her attention, all her efforts really meant.

"It's true, Harper—you're really a great friend."

And that was Adam—hopelessly oblivious, as always.

But so painfully perfect, in every other way.

She closed her eyes for a moment, imagining what it might be like to open them to a different world, one in which Adam was sitting across the table gazing at her in that way, that tender awestruck way that had always been reserved for Beth. If she could just get him to really *look* at her, to see what he was missing. She raised a hand to her neck, let her fingers play their way down the bare skin until they reached her silky neckline—if she opened her eyes, would she catch him sneaking a forbidden glance, wondering what lay beneath?

She opened her eyes.

And the answer was no.

He wasn't even looking in her direction—he'd turned toward the door, toward a gaggle of girls from their school who had just walked in. Toward Kaia. Of course.

And there went her perfect night, her golden opportunity.

Kaia spotted them, raised an arm in greeting, and treated Adam to a long, slow smile. Harper just sneered. And waited.

Adam paused for a moment, nodded briefly in acknowledgment—and then turned away.

Harper breathed a sigh of relief, and only then realized that she'd been holding her breath, tensed and ready for rejection. But Adam was still there, and Kaia—one eyebrow

raised in—surprise? Skepticism? Disbelief? Whatever—
Kaia sat down across the bar.

Good. And you'd better stay there, Harper thought. She
resisted the impulse to make some snide comment about her
nemesis—or about the fact that Adam seemed suddenly
to have abandoned his Siamese twin act and was actually
allowing some space to intrude between him and his illicit
beloved.

No reason to ruin a perfect moment—even for the
perfect snark.

Besides, the important thing was that he was staying
away. Whatever the reason, Kaia had lost this round—she
was across the bar and Harper was here, across from Adam.

Across from his deep blue eyes and luscious smile and
biceps that could—

"Harper, there's—there's something I need to talk to
you about."

That's it—no more gazing, no more dreaming, she told herself sternly. *Must stay focused. Listen.* Even though he was
looking at her so intently—was, unbelievably, leaning in
close and laying his hand on top of hers. Even though it
was hard not to lose herself in the electrifying contact and
in fantasies of where this might be going. . . . No. Must
focus. Pay attention. Hope.

"You've always said I could talk to you about anything," he began hesitantly.

Harper just nodded, afraid, for once, to speak.

"Well . . . you know that Beth and I have been really
happy together, that I think she's wonderful. . . ."

His voice trailed off, and Harper nodded again, impatiently. There was only so much of this she could listen to,

and if the evening was about to devolve into yet another monologue about Beth's million-and-one divine attributes, she was going to need a *lot* more to drink.

"And I mean, she is wonderful," he continued, "but . . ."

But? That was more like it.

"Well, this last week I've just been—"

"Harper! Harper! Over here!"

Oh God, not now.

Distracted by the shrill voice, Adam broke off what he was saying, and they both looked up to see a pale, skinny girl waving frantically from a few tables away.

"Harper! Look, we're here too!"

A ditzy blond sophomore who'd decided last spring to make Harper her role model, life trainer, and personal guru, whether Harper liked it or not.

It wasn't enough that the girl followed her around so much at school that Harper had dubbed her "Mini-Me"? She had to follow Harper *here,* too? Had to ruin what might have been her perfect night?

"Just ignore her," she urged Adam. "What were you about to say?"

Adam paused, then laughed nervously. "You know what? Forget it."

"But—"

"No, you go talk to your friends—I'm heading off to the bathroom." He grinned. "You'll still be around when I get back, though, right?"

"I don't know, Adam." Harper looked pointedly at the next table over, where a middle-aged guy with too much stomach and too few teeth was chugging his beer, soggy cigarette lodged firmly in the corner of his mouth. "Lots of hot prospects around here—once you disappear, who knows who I'll find. . . ."

He laughed, and Harper forced herself to join in. But as soon as he turned away, her face turned to ice. What if, when Adam came back, he'd lost his nerve, and never said whatever it was he'd been about to tell her? She couldn't believe that one loser with bad timing had just torpedoed her moment—and here came Mini-Me now, dragging along her equally bland best friend, aka Mini-She.

Both apparently gluttons for punishment.

"Hey, Harper, didn't you see us over there? I can't believe that you're here too!" Mini-Me gushed.

"Isn't the band great?" Mini-She asked excitedly.

"Yeah, and the lead singer is so hot—don't you think?" Mini-Me added.

Harper looked up on stage, where scruffy Reed Sawyer, stoner, sixth-year senior, wannabe badass, all-around burnout—and lead singer of the Blind Monkeys—was torturing a guitar with only slightly less incompetence than the rest of his band of losers.

"I think love must be blind *and* deaf," Harper drawled.

The girls looked back at her blankly.

Harper was undecided. Despite their utter clueless-ness and stalker tendencies, she rarely went out of her way to torture these girls—not out of pity or virtue, but because they were embarrassingly easy targets. On the other hand, as demonstrated by tonight's disaster, her tol-erance had apparently been a hideous mistake. . . .

"Hey, you know who else is here?" Mini-Me asked.

"Britney Spears?" Harper guessed.

"No way—but how cool would that be?!" Mini-Me

said. Apparently she'd been absent the day sarcasm genes were handed out. "No—*Kaia's* here! And you should see what she's wearing—she says it's from *Dolce and Gabbana*."

"*So* cool," Mini-She sighed appreciatively.

Harper rolled her eyes, taking only minimal joy in the fact that her little friends had apparently intruded on the new girl's night too. The last thing she needed right now was a Kaia lovefest. Enough was enough.

"You know, the scene here is getting kind of lame," Harper confided. "I think pretty soon I'm going to head out to this party I heard about. You should—oh wait, no, they probably wouldn't let you in."

"What?"

"Where?"

"A party?"

Good, she'd hooked them. Now, to reel them in. "Yeah, some college guys who haven't gone back to school yet," she continued. "They're set up in this old warehouse along the highway."

"No way!" Mini-Me said breathlessly. "So . . . think we could come with you?"

"Well . . . I probably shouldn't even have told you about it." The girls looked crestfallen. "But since I have . . ." She pretended to stop and think for a moment, and then, "Hey, why not? If I give you the password, they should let you in."

Harper wrote down an address and "password" on a napkin and surreptitiously passed it to the girls. "You shouldn't wait for me, though—I have to stick around here for a while to take care of Adam." She leaned in and lowered her voice. "Don't tell anyone, but he and Beth had another fight."

There, that should get the gossip chain started and hope-fully put a nice shiny nail in the coffin of that relationship.

"But you know what," Harper said, smiling at her own bright idea, "why don't you invite Kaia along? I'm sure she'd love to see what a good party looks like around here—and she certainly won't want to spend the rest of her night in this dump."

"Thanks, Harper, that's a great idea," Mini-Me enthused. "You're really the best, you know that?"

Harper just smiled. "Actually, I do."

The girls took off, and Harper watched them as they headed back to their table and collected their stuff. Looked like they were taking the bait. She felt a momentary twinge of guilt at the thought of them wandering through a dark and empty warehouse wondering where the frat boys were and where the keg was hidden—but Harper didn't believe in rewarding stupidity with leniency. And at least this way they would learn their lesson.

Maybe.

Now if only they could drag Kaia along with them. She peered through the crowd to check out Kaia's table—but Kaia was gone. Home for the night? It seemed unlikely that such a wild party girl—or so she claimed—would have given up on the nightlife so early, pathetic as it was. More likely, she was off somewhere looking for trouble.

Speaking of which . . . Adam had been gone forever, and the bathroom just wasn't that far away.

So where was he?

"You know you want me," Kaia whispered, her breath hot and moist against his ear.

Adam said nothing, but didn't—couldn't—push her away.

He'd pushed her away in the motel room—and she'd come back.

He'd pushed her away in the locker room—and she'd come back.

He'd pushed her away when she accosted him outside the bathroom—and yet she was still here. Still had her arms wrapped around him.

He was so tired of pushing.

And she was so beautiful.

It amazed him—how Kaia and Beth could be so different, how Kaia could be the opposite of almost everything he loved about Beth (and he did love her, he reminded himself, reassured himself). Kaia was hard where Beth was soft, confident where Beth was shy, determined where Beth was so easily deterred. Kaia's jet black hair, her sparkling green eyes, her icy beauty—they were nothing like the silky blond comfort he found in Beth's arms.

So different, and yet—

And yet he wanted them both so much.

But Beth would never forgive him.

"Beth would never have to know," she whispered, as if she'd read his thoughts.

Or had he spoken them aloud?

Adam no longer knew. Kaia's perfume washed over him, mixing with the smoky air, and he was suffocating, he was dizzy, he was lost in the pounding of the music, the vibrations running through the floor, through their bodies, the thunderous bass. He was lost in the sight of her swollen lips, her wide eyes, her body pressing against his in the darkness.

He thought of Beth, of the look on her face when she'd walked away from him outside the school, of the sound of her voice through her tears, telling him she didn't trust him, could never trust him. He thought of what Beth would think, what she would do if she saw him here with Kaia. Thought of proving her wrong, thought of proving her right—

And then, as Kaia's hands tightened around his waist, as his chest pressed against hers, as her tongue slipped past his lips—he wasn't thinking about Beth anymore.

She should never have gone looking for him.

That was all Harper could think, the only words her mind could muster as she stood frozen, staring at the two of them. Together. Wrapped in each other's arms.

Harper wanted to say something—wanted to spit out a venomous one-liner that would make them leap apart in shame. She wanted to shoot them both a murderous look, then shrug her shoulders, spin on her heel, and walk off in disgust.

A perfect exit.

Classy.

Cool.

Unconcerned.

But she had no words—she'd lost the power to speak, to stalk away. It was all she could do to keep standing, breathing . . . watching.

And so, paralyzed, half-hidden by the darkness—not that either of them would have noticed her had she been lit up by a spotlight—she stayed, wanting nothing more than to turn away. But couldn't.

Couldn't stop watching him, his hands running through her hair, his lips pressed against hers, her hands running up and down his back, then their hands clasped, their fingers intertwined—Kaia's hands, Kaia's fingers, Kaia's lips where she had always dreamed that hers would, should be. . . .

No.

Harper took a deep breath and forced herself to turn her back on the couple, on her best friend, on what the night could have been. Turned away.

She would not cry. No matter what, she would not cry—and she would not stay.

She pushed her way through the smoky bar and threw herself out into the cool desert night.

Let him wonder where she'd gone.

Let him find his own ride home.

And—she knew he would.

Hating her, hating him—hating herself for being so weak, for being so pathetic, for not being able to hate him at all—not even now, when the two of them, together, all over each other, was all she could see, Harper walked aimlessly down the empty street.

She was shaking, but she didn't feel the cold—could feel nothing, except the painful, empty hole in the pit of her stomach. Her bare hand, which had so recently been warmed by his touch. And finally, after a few blocks and a few deep breaths, the rage. The hot blaze of anger—and the cool certainty that this was not over, that this was not a fight she was prepared to lose.

Adam would be hers . . . and Kaia would be sorry.

They went back to the abandoned motel. Of course.

Adam felt like he was watching the scene happen to someone else. That couldn't be him, clutching Kaia's hand, following her down the long and dusty hallways and into one of the cramped, dark rooms. It must be someone else giving in to her warm touch, the soft pressure of her hands forcing him down onto the mattress. It couldn't be him.

All his willpower had drifted away, all the excitement and energy that had surged through him in the club as he finally let himself go and ran his hands over her body, as she nibbled his earlobe and whispered, "Let's get out of here"—all that had seeped away. This wasn't a crime committed in the heat of passion—it was a crime of omission, a failure to stop the chain of events that had started in the bar, that had brought him here.

But who could stop an avalanche? Who could stop a train wreck?

Inevitability.

That was the word he was groping for. Everything had taken on a strange tinge of inevitability, as if everything that had happened in the last few weeks, everything since he'd first seen her, first taken her hand in his, had led directly to this moment. To Kaia.

She stood before him and, with a sultry smile, pulled off her halter top, revealing the black lace bra that lay beneath.

Then off went the shimmering silver skirt.

Off went the lace.

She crawled into bed beside him.

"Your turn," she whispered, and began unbuttoning his jeans.

A warm heat flushed through him and he felt his lost passion returning—and along with it, his doubt.

"Kaia," he said softly, allowing her to pull his T-shirt over his head, to kiss her way across his bare chest as his hands, as if of their own accord, massaged the soft contours of her body. "Kaia, I'm not sure we should . . ."

"Shh," she whispered, stopping him with a kiss. "Don't worry, I'll be gentle."

And off went the boxers.

chapter

12

The phone rang and rang, but there was no answer. As the voice mail kicked in again, Adam hung up in disgust. He'd left too many messages, and his voice was beginning to take on a distinct tinge of desperation. But where was she?

(*Screening your calls,* his inner voice whispered. He ignored it.)

He needed to talk to her, needed to see her—and for what? He didn't even know. When he'd woken up this morning, the whole thing, the foggy memory of their bodies wrapped together, of their feverish wrestling, thrusting, caressing, moaning—it had all seemed like a dream.

But it had happened.

And it could never happen again—except that there was nothing he wanted more than to see her, to touch her, to feel her hands all over him.

Guilt burned through him every time he thought about what he'd done, and he thought about it constantly. And maybe the pain of guilt was worth it.

He decided to go outside, shoot some hoops, burn off some nervous energy. His mother had yet to return home from her own escapades the night before, and the house was too empty, too quiet. He didn't want to face anyone else—not now that he had a secret that was weighing down on him so heavily. Besides, normal human interaction might bring him back down to Earth, penetrate the haze that seemed to lay over him, that gave every moment a heightened clarity, every sensation a powerful charge. He felt different, somehow, and he wasn't ready to share the feeling—or to lose it. He didn't want to be alone with his thoughts, though—well, more than anything, he wanted to be alone with his thoughts and his fantasies, but that seemed too dangerous. Because the more he thought, the more he wanted.

He changed into a ratty T-shirt and some running shorts, grabbed the ball out of the garage, and jogged over to the driveway. It was a blisteringly hot day, the heat billowing up in waves from the black concrete. Good. Maybe he could sweat out this disease that Kaia had infected him with, this bottomless craving for her body, for the feel of her skin against him. He needed to stop thinking about her, to stop thinking at all, to just focus on the feeling of his muscles straining in exertion, his feet pounding the ground, his hands on the ball, sending it flying toward the basket. He would lose himself in the moment.

He brought the phone outside with him, though. Just in case.

Adam didn't know how long he was out there, dribbling, racing back and forth across the length of the driveway, trying to force himself into an oblivion of exhaustion. It almost worked. Finally he stopped, out of breath and every muscle screaming. He bent forward, letting his arms dangle freely toward the ground, then straightened up and dumped a bottle of water over his head.

And there was the phone, lying on the ground, taunting him with its silence. He wrestled with himself, then slammed the ball into the pavement in frustration. It bounced with a resounding thud; Adam scooped it up with one hand—with the other he picked up the phone. He flipped it open, just in case he'd been so in the zone that he'd missed a call. But he hadn't.

And then, as he shuffled up the walkway toward his front door, it rang in his hands. Startled, Adam fumbled it for a moment, almost dropped it—dropped the ball instead—and finally flipped it open to check the caller ID.

Beth.

She'd been calling all weekend.

He flipped the phone shut again, ignoring the tension creeping through his body. For now, at least, what was there to say?

The phone rang and rang, but Harper didn't even bother to see who it was, much less consider answering it.

It would be Miranda, of course, as it had been the last twenty times, calling to see where she'd disappeared to, wondering what had happened Friday night. Harper's mouth twisted into a sour grin—maybe Miranda was imagining her and Adam holed away in the bedroom together, an isolated lovers' tryst. Right.

The first few calls, she'd raced to the phone, expecting it to be Adam, begging for forgiveness. Not that she would have answered, she reminded herself—but there would have been a certain satisfaction in listening to his voice on the machine, groveling for mercy.

Saturday had passed, and most of Sunday—and the call had never come.

She would like to think that he was in his bedroom even now, staring out the window at her house, too racked with guilt to call her, too afraid of what her response might be. Agonizing over whether he'd thrown away a twelve-year friendship for a one-night stand.

Somehow, she doubted it.

She knew all she had to do was pick up the phone and Miranda would appear, complete with the requisite care package of trashy chick flicks and a bottle of Absolut. Miranda had a secret stash hidden in an old suitcase under her bed for moments just like this. She could easily have slipped a couple of bottles out of the house and spent the weekend over at Harper's, under the guise of keeping Harper company while her parents were out of town. She knew she should have called Miranda at some point, regardless, as the two of them had arranged to meet at the Cedar Creek Motel earlier that day to supervise the team of sophomores that Harper had suckered into cleaning the place. (They'd been sworn to secrecy about the location but offered admittance to the party—*if* their Lysol and vacuuming efforts were deemed up to snuff.) Too bad. Miranda would just have to take care of it alone or leave the sophomores to fend for themselves. She'd be pissed off, but Harper knew she would understand—there were plenty of extenuating circumstances.

And Harper just wanted to be alone. Her mother had dragged her father off for a weekend of "antiquing"—both he and Harper knew this was code for "digging through unwanted, flea-infested crap at roadside junk sales," but neither had much desire to puncture Amanda Grace's illusions. Harper's mother spent her time in a world of her own making, one that was infinitely richer, more elegant, more high society, more *appropriate* than the dirty present, in which the Grace family, once lords of the manor, now struggled to keep their heads above water.

But Harper was trapped in the harsh reality of the present: an empty house, empty hours to fill. As the phone began to ring again, Harper moaned and pulled one of the couch pillows over her head to drown out the noise. She'd been self-medicating with vodka and cookie dough, but forty-eight hours of that had only left her with a persistent thudding headache and periodic waves of nausea. In a few hours she would crawl into bed, hide under the covers, and pass out, trying not to think about waking up Monday morning and facing the world.

Struggle with a smile, she thought. It was her mother's cardinal rule. Do whatever you need to do—but never let them see you cry.

Kaia shut off her phone.

She was sick of seeing Adam's name pop up on the caller ID what seemed like every five minutes—and face it, it's not like anyone else would be trying to call.

She shuffled down to the kitchen to snag another pint of Ben and Jerry's. When she'd arrived in town a few weeks ago, the refrigerator and freezer had been completely empty, the sparkling stainless steel kitchen with its state-of-the-art appliances virtually unused. Typical bachelor pad. Even though the bachelor in question was a fifty-two-year-old defense contractor with two ex-wives and a seventeen-year-old daughter. Kaia didn't know what her father had been eating—it's not like there were a lot of takeout options in town, and she somehow didn't see Keith Sellers pulling his BMW sedan into the Nifty Fifties lot on a regular basis.

Since she'd arrived, she'd had the cook stock up on her favorite foods—at least the ones that could be purchased nearby or shipped in—and, after so many years of nonstop restaurant cuisine, she had to admit that night after night of home-cooked meals was actually a welcome change. Even if she did usually eat her gourmet food spread out on a TV table in the den—the dining room was too large and impersonal for one. And one was the most she ever got.

Anyway, she'd sent the cook home for the weekend, and instead of her usual diet of whole grains, soy, and fresh greens, she was treating herself to a couple of days of soggy pizza and Ben and Jerry's. Why not? Hadn't she accomplished her mission? Didn't she deserve a little reward?

Kaia scooped some Chubby Hubby into a ceramic bowl (ecru colored, to match the walls) and squeezed some chocolate sauce on top. Perfect. Grabbing a spoon, she headed back into the living room and settled onto the couch, just in time for the beginning of a "very special" Lifetime movie. Like all Lifetime movies, it was a cautionary tale of teen pregnancy or anorexia or domestic violence or something—Kaia didn't really care. She just liked to watch all the fucked-up people sort out their problems in such reliably melodramatic ways. And it helped kill the time.

"You're grounded!" her father had shouted in exasperation when she'd strolled in the door a little before dawn.

She'd just smirked. Grounded? As if that were a punishment in a place like this—as if there were anywhere else in this town she'd rather be than on her couch, watching shitty movies. Grace was nothing but tedium. Which her father might have known if he'd spent more than five minutes with her since she'd come to town. But no—he'd swooped home on the *one* night she was out until dawn, freaked out, grounded her, then disappeared before she woke up the next morning. Off he went on another "business trip," along with his omnipresent personal assistant, who, conveniently, looked like a low-rent Playboy Bunny.

As if the maid was really going to enforce the whole grounding thing if Kaia decided to leave the house. In fact, Kaia realized, it would almost be worth the trouble of venturing out, just to force the confrontation. . . .

Almost, but not quite.

No, on Monday morning she'd go back to work, so to speak—continue her pursuit of Jack Powell, enjoy the taste of her conquest over Adam, sit back to watch the chaos that would inevitably ensue. And if anyone asked, she would describe a whirlwind jaunt to Manhattan, a jet-setting weekend filled with star-studded parties and risqué encounters—much like the weekend she was sure all her East Coast "friends" were currently sleeping off. Not that any of them would bother to tell her about it—or take a break from the high life and visit her in exile.

But no one had to know that. She turned up the volume on the TV—it was anorexia this time, with an "all star cast" featuring some guy from *7th Heaven* and that woman from *The Facts of Life* (she showed up in 70 percent of all Lifetime movies—and Kaia would know).

It was a guilty pleasure, Kaia acknowledged, scarfing down another spoonful of her ice cream. Embarrassing, yes—but all in all not such a bad way to spend a weekend.

chapter

13

By Monday, Adam had less of a grip than ever on what he wanted to say to Kaia—he just knew that he needed to talk to her, needed to see her, needed it more with every passing minute. The guilt of what they'd done was crushing him; he'd managed to avoid Beth all day long, but his luck couldn't last forever. Even so, his nightmarish visions of what might happen were far less vivid than his impassioned memories of what *had* happened, and . . .

And basically, he was completely confused.

"Kaia!" he called, finally spotting her glossy black hair in the crowd as the final bell echoed through the halls. "Kaia, wait up a minute!" He jogged to catch up with her, breaking into a bright smile as she turned to face him. She was wearing a form-fitting black shirt that laced up the front and jeans so tight they could have been painted on. The indecision and complexities of a moment ago seemed to melt away.

"Adam." She sighed. "What is it?"

"Where were you all weekend?" he asked, hoping not to sound too desperate. He was, he reminded himself, a superstar on this campus. He was beloved by the masses, adored by throngs of girls. He shouldn't need to be chasing one through the halls, even if she was so beautiful it hurt, even if her touch made him forget that there'd ever been anyone else. *No* girl was worth humiliating himself. And yet—he heard the panic creeping into his voice. And couldn't stop it. "Didn't you get my messages?"

"I was away," she said shortly. "Back in New York. So what did you want?"

"I wanted—" Adam broke off. What did he want? That was the whole problem, wasn't it? He wanted her, of course, right here, right now. But didn't he also want to be with Beth, his sweet, innocent girlfriend? Other than the awkwardly mumbled hellos exchanged at their neighboring lockers, they hadn't spoken in almost a week, which was the longest time in months he'd gone without hearing from her. And he missed her, he did—but it was hard to remember that when his eyes, without his permission, remained riveted on Kaia's deep red lips.

He pulled her out of the path of the crowd and into a small alcove behind the lockers and lowered his voice. He'd just make it up as he went along.

"I wanted to talk to you," he said urgently.

"So you got me. Talk about what?"

About what? What else?

"About, you know, about what we *did*," he whispered, darting his head around to make sure no one could overhear. "About what we're going to do about it."

About whether we're going to do it again.

"What's there to *do* about it?" she asked, sounding mystified. "Or to talk about? We did it, and"—she touched his cheek briefly, gently—"it was great. But, you know, it's done. What do you want from me?"

Adam was stunned. "I just thought we could—well, you'd said—and when we were at the motel—I just thought you wanted—"

Kaia laughed—it was a musical sound, lighter and more spontaneous than anything he'd seen her say or do in the short time they'd known each other. That was the difference, he suddenly realized: This was real—and everything else had all been calculated.

"Oh, Adam," she said, her voice dripping with a patronizing sympathy. "What? Did you think we were going to *date* or something? Were you thinking this was going to be a *relationship*?" She pronounced the word as if it tasted rotten coming out of her mouth.

Then she laughed again, and Adam finally got it. He may have been slow, but he wasn't stupid.

"Whatever," he said brusquely. "I just wanted to be sure that you didn't get the wrong idea. I'm with Beth, you know. I love her." The familiar phrase sounded unconvincing, even to him. Especially to him.

"I know you do," Kaia assured him, grinning brightly now. "So you must be pretty terrified that she'll find out about this, hmm?" She gave him a cryptic look. "But hey, who would tell her?"

Shit. Adam had never before understood what it would feel like to have one's heart leap into one's throat. Now he knew. It felt like your chest was an empty shell about to collapse in on itself. It felt like strong hands had wrapped themselves around your neck, squeezing like a vise, choking the air out of you. He saw it clearly now, every step of her—what, her plan? Seduction. Betrayal. All that, just to get him into bed? Or to make him feel like a fool? Or was the true prize whatever was about to come next, all hell breaking loose when Beth learned the truth? Would anyone really go to so much effort, just to cause themselves a little pleasure—or someone else so much pain?

"Kaia," he said warningly, "you wouldn't—"

Who, me? she mimed, the picture of innocence.

"I'm hurt," she said aloud. "Don't you know me at all by now?" She gave him a quick peck on the cheek and skipped off down the hallway. "You know you can trust me!" she called over her shoulder.

He was so totally screwed.

"So which one do you like better?"

Silence.

"Beth? Beth? You still with me?"

Beth stared at the newspaper layout sheets with the same blank gaze she'd been aiming at the world for days. Ever since she'd caught Adam with Kaia outside the locker room, ever since she'd blown up at him and run away, she'd been a little bit lost. The first couple of days hadn't been so bad, as she'd been riding a wave of anger that swept away any lingering doubts or concerns. She'd avoided him in the hallways, she'd ditched out on their date—and, while working behind the counter at the diner, she'd pretended the tomatoes and onions were his head, and spent a pleasant hour chopping him to pieces, over and over again.

But after that—well, she was still mad, but she was a little mad at herself, too. She was ready to kiss and make up—but Adam, it seemed, was too busy to take her calls. She'd spent all weekend trying to track him down, stealing a few minutes from her shift to sneak off with a cell phone; bribing her little brothers into shutting up long enough to make a phone call; taking breaks every ten minutes from her stacks of homework to check her phone, see if he'd called. No.

Maybe this was it, she'd decided after a fitful night of sleep. She'd screwed up the best thing she had in her life—though, if he was willing to let go that easily, maybe it wasn't something worth fighting for after all.

"What?" Beth suddenly realized that Jack Powell, sitting across from her in the newspaper office, was holding up two layout sheets in front of her and waiting for some kind of response. Too bad she had no idea what he had asked. "Oh, sorry—uh, yeah, that looks fine."

Jack Powell laid the sheets down on the desk and turned in his chair to look at Beth head-on.

"Beth, is everything okay?" he asked with concern. "You've been a little out of it all afternoon—if there's somewhere else you'd rather be . . . ?"

"No!" she cried in alarm. Sitting here with Mr. Powell, she felt almost secure again, almost calm, for the first time in days. Yes, she was still thinking about Adam constantly, working through their fight again and again, trying to see where everything had gone so wrong—but somehow, having Jack there, droning on in his delicious voice about column space or layouts or whatever, made everything seem a little more manageable. Today he was wearing a stylish button-down shirt, with colorful vertical stripes running down its length—it made him look years younger. Good thing he's not, Beth pointed out to herself, or sitting in this small, dark room with him, facing him across the table, our heads leaning in together, our hands brushing past each other to dig through the piles of papers—it would be a whole different story. One her boyfriend wouldn't like very much.

Then she remembered she might not have a boyfriend anymore, and the thought hit her with a stinging pain that brought tears to her eyes. She took a few deep breaths and looked away from Mr. Powell for a moment, calming herself down.

"No," she finally repeated in a steadier voice. "There's really nowhere I'd rather be. I just—I'm just having a little trouble concentrating today. That's all."

"Well, that's obvious," he said sympathetically. "Here's a radical idea—want to talk about it?"

Beth cringed. Talk about her love life with a teacher? A teacher she just happened to have an absurdly large crush on? Didn't seem like the best idea.

"I know it's weird, since I'm your teacher," he said, reading her mind. He placed a tentative hand on hers. "But Beth, I'd really like to be your friend, too."

Maybe it was the warmth in his voice, or the soft pressure of his hand, but something inside of Beth just broke.

"It's my boyfriend," she said, choking back the tears. Powell nodded encouragingly. "Things have been weird lately, and we're fighting all the time, and now he's not speaking to me and I just—"

She broke off and buried her face in her arms, hiding the humiliating tears.

She felt a gentle hand on her back and, instinctively, tensed up.

"Beth," he said firmly. "Beth, sit up, look at me—you don't have to be embarrassed."

She reluctantly straightened and faced him. He pulled a light blue handkerchief out of his pocket and offered it to her—even in her dismay, she could appreciate the chivalry. She blew into it noisily, wiped the tears away from her eyes, then sat still, taking some deep breaths and twisting the soft cloth nervously in her hands.

"I think I may have ruined everything," she murmured, knowing from the look in his eyes that he understood.

Jack Powell shook his head.

"Beth, Beth, Beth, it's not you, it's him. I promise you that."

"How do you know?"

"Difficult as it may be to imagine, I was a teenage boy once. Trust me, we're all idiots."

Distraught as she was, Beth managed a small smile.

"No, I'm sure whoever this boy is," he continued, "whatever the problem is, he's being an idiot. He's just a boy. But you, Beth," he paused, looking her up and down appraisingly. "You're a woman. A beautiful, intelligent, kindhearted *woman*."

Beth flushed furiously, and her eyes darted around the room; she was unsure where to look, what to do, faced with words like that from a man like him.

"He can't give you what you need, Beth," he told her, slowly running a hand through her long blond hair. She wanted to pull away but didn't. "You need maturity, understanding, passion," he continued. "This guy doesn't deserve you."

She looked down at the table, but then he said her name again and when she looked up, his handsome face was right there, inches from hers and moving closer, and his hands were on her, drawing her in, and then their lips met and he held her to him.

"Oh, Beth," he murmured, and his lips were on her again, his tongue pushing its way into her mouth before she knew what was happening, exploring the moist, dark spaces inside of her, his hands running up and down her back—

She pushed him away, hard, jumped out of her seat and began backing toward the door.

"What are you—? Mr. Powell, what . . . ?"

But she knew what. And she wanted to throw up, wanted to scrub the taste of him out of her mouth, wanted to fly at him, pound his chest with her fists, tear at his face with her nails, knock that bemused look off his poisonously handsome face. But instead she just stood in the doorway, unable to take a step forward—or back.

He started toward her. "Beth, I'm sorry, calm down, just sit down for a moment," he pleaded.

He held his arms out from his sides, a conciliatory gesture, and gave her a weak half smile—it grew wider as she remained unmoving, then took a hesitant step toward him. He looked so stricken and apologetic, and after all, hadn't he just done exactly what she'd been dreaming of him doing all these weeks? Maybe, Beth realized, horrified, she'd sent out some kind of signal, had drawn him in, overwhelmed his common sense—maybe she was the one who'd ruined everything.

"Come back in," he repeated, "and we'll talk about it. Everything will be fine."

More talk. But that's how it had all started—and after what had just happened, what was she supposed to say?

Beth shook her head, tears streaming freely down her face. She opened her mouth as if to speak, then closed it again.

And ran out of the room.

Kaia pressed herself into the shadows, shaking with anger.

Beth, blinded by tears, ran by without seeing her. Kaia would deal with her later.

For now: Jack Powell. The asshole, the liar.

After blowing off Adam, she'd come to take another after-hours crack at the French teacher, hoping to convince him that rules were made to be broken.

But apparently, he already knew that.

She stood outside his doorway and watched as he took a few halfhearted steps after Beth, then sighed and slumped back down into his chair. He tapped an index finger rhythmically against his lips, looked up at the empty doorway, and then checked his watch—as if wondering whether she would come back, and how long he should choose to wait.

Don't hold your breath, Kaia thought, shivering in disgust as the image of him lunging at Beth flashed through her mind. The girl (who'd obviously been mooning over Powell for weeks) was clearly either too wimpy or too stupid to take him up on the offer.

Kaia could see what he'd been thinking, of course. A girl like Beth would be easy to push around—she wasn't "trouble in a miniskirt." He'd probably guessed that she would jump at the chance to play his dutiful concubine for the year, rescuing him from boredom and then sweetly and quietly disappearing when the time came.

Kaia almost laughed—apparently, he'd guessed wrong. She was about to enter the room and blast Powell for spurning her, taunt him with what she knew. Then she stopped, considering his stooped figure—chin resting on his fists, staring into the distance, maybe wondering how to clean up the mess he'd made for himself if it ever came to light. If.

Kaia guessed that he was probably congratulating himself for picking a girl like Beth, who would likely lack the backbone needed to get him into any trouble. He probably figured that by steering clear of Kaia, by refusing to indulge in any "inappropriate fraternization" with the troublemaker, he would at least be safe on that front. At least he'd dodged that bullet.

Kaia shook her head in pity, and this time, she did laugh.

Sorry, Mr. Powell. Wrong again.

They ran into each other at their lockers—they were next to each other, of course. Midway through last year, Adam had bribed some sophomore to switch with him, so that he and Beth could be side by side. Sometimes Beth slipped little love notes in through the ventilation cracks at the top, and once in a while, Adam had even thought to make a romantic gesture of his own. On Valentine's Day he had papered the inside of her locker with cut-out construction paper hearts and left a bouquet of roses waiting for her. It had always been a good thing, having the same home base to come back to, an easy meeting point, a safe refuge in the busy chaos of the day. But having neighboring lockers also meant there was no escape, and so here they were, side by side, at the worst possible time.

Still wet from swim practice and still steaming from his run-in with Kaia, Adam slammed his locker open and grabbed his bag, accidentally knocking down the photo of Beth he'd taped to the inside of the door on the first day of school. A spasm of guilt shot through him, and he snatched the picture off the ground, trying to stick it back up, but it was no use. The tape was too dried out, and he was forced to lay the picture atop a pile of junk; he swore to himself that he'd bring in more tape the next day and make things right. He'd make everything right.

He slammed the door shut, giving it a kick for good measure, and cursed Kaia under his breath, not for the first time.

The soulless, manipulative bitch.

And he'd let her ruin his life.

Enter Beth.

Tearful, replaying the moment in her mind again and again, and yet still unable to believe it had actually happened.

And had she wanted it to happen?

Asked for it to happen?

He saw her first—and had almost enough time to shrink away. But not quite.

"Beth!" he said forcefully. "I've been looking for you all day."

"Adam?" Beth, who had walked right past him without noticing and began slowly spinning the combination lock on her locker, looked up hesitantly. It was as if she didn't recognize him, didn't quite believe he was real. Maybe because she'd already been imagining him standing there, because right now there was no one in the world she wanted to see more—or less.

She closed her eyes and took a moment of silence to shut out the world and regroup—but when she opened them, he was still there, waiting.

"Adam, I, uh . . ." her voice trailed off. What was she supposed to do, forget about their fight, tell him the truth about what had just happened, send him off to beat up Jack Powell and then get thrown out of school? And, of course, he'd never look at her the same way again. The Beth he knew didn't go around seducing teachers—no, if she was going to make this work, she had to remain the girl he'd fallen in love with, and that girl was innocent, trustworthy, and above all, loyal. She didn't need anyone other than her boyfriend, even in her fantasies.

And that's who I am, she reminded herself. *I* am *that girl.*

"I'm sorry," he finally said, breaking the silence.

"I want to apologize," she sputtered at the same time.

And that was all it took.

They spoke at once, the words spilling out hesitantly, their words overlapping, their voices growing in speed and strength as they decided where they were going, drowning each other out in their eagerness to get there.

"No, I'm sorry, I don't know what I was thinking."

"I've been horrible."

"I should have called—"

"I just wanted to say—"

"I missed you—"

"I love you—"

They stammered, and babbled, and then, finally, they embraced.

Adam held her tight, breathing in the fresh, clean scent of her hair. Thinking, *She can never find out.*

Beth dug her fingers into his flesh, wishing she would never have to let go. Deciding, *He can never know.*

They stayed like that, frozen in the empty hallway, for several long minutes, leaning on each other. Two minds with a single, desperate thought: *This time, I'll make it work. This time, I have to.*

She was lying in bed, stumbling haplessly through her math homework, when she heard it. His car, pulling into the driveway, a loud rumbling and clinking that could belong to no one but Bertha the beat-up Chevy. She would know it anywhere.

Harper flipped the book shut and leaped to her feet, creeping over to the window—there was nothing wrong with taking a quick look at him, she told herself. Just because she wasn't speaking to him (not that he'd seemed to notice—it probably didn't even count as the silent treatment if she hadn't actually seen him face-to-face yet and had the chance to snub him) didn't mean she couldn't watch from afar, just to see what he was doing. Who he was with.

The car pulled to a stop and Adam jumped out, walked slowly around to the passenger's side, and held the door open. A blond head appeared, and he put his arm around her waist.

Harper couldn't actually make out the girl's face from her perch, but who needed to? She should have guessed this would happen. Adam and Beth walked together up the pathway toward the front door, his hand still resting on her back, her head against his shoulder. Harper couldn't bring herself to look away. He unlocked his front door, but they paused before stepping inside—Adam cradled Beth's face in his hands and turned it up toward him. And they kissed.

That was more than enough.

Harper shut her blinds in disgust and flung herself back down on the bed. This was getting ridiculous. First she had to watch Adam getting it on with Kaia in public, right in front of her—on *her* date, no less. Then, just when she'd finally decided to embrace the silver lining (i.e., the imminent demise of Beth and Adam's lovers' paradise), he pulls into his driveway and heads inside with Little Miss Perfect herself in tow.

Was Adam hooking up with everyone in town but Harper?

It was beginning to feel that way.

chapter

14

"Remember when we used to play GI Joes out here?" Adam asked lazily, lying back on the large, flat rock and staring up at the stars.

So he hadn't apologized. So what? After a few days Harper's anger had burned down to a low simmer, and with Beth back in the picture and Kaia up to God knows what, Harper didn't have time to waste sulking in a corner. If she was going to win Adam, she was going to have to get in the game. *Besides,* she thought, looking fondly over at her oldest friend, lying next to her on the cool granite, *it was Adam.* Too dense to realize he'd done something wrong, so what was even the point in making him feel guilty? Especially when he called out of the blue with a mysterious request to meet him outside, at *their* place, to talk about some "stuff." When he needed her, she was there—that's just how it worked.

"I remember when *I* used to play GI Joes while *you*

spent most of your time with my Barbie collection," Harper teased him.

"Hey, Barbie was hot!" Adam protested.

Harper rolled her eyes. "Right, and *that's* why you used to beg me to let you dress her up and drive her around in the Barbie Corvette." She propped herself up slightly to give him a close look at her skeptical expression. "You just keep telling yourself that."

"I slept with her, Harper."

She froze, still facing him, and it took every ounce of strength she had to keep her face still. No eyes widening in shock or horror, no mouth turning down in disappointment, no tears or telltale blushing—she just looked at him steadily and concentrated on remembering to breathe.

"Who, Barbie?" she asked, narrowly managing to keep her voice light. She let some of the tension leach out of her muscles and sank back onto the smooth surface of the rock.

"Kaia. I'm serious, Harper. I slept with her." He made a strange keening noise, half between a groan and a yelp. "What the hell am I supposed to do now?"

Get yourself checked out for STDs?

But Harper bit back the comment and was glad for the darkness—it gave her a place to hide.

So he'd slept with her. At least now she knew.

Though she wished she didn't.

"So that's why we're out here?" Harper asked. Though she'd suspected as much. The rock bridged the boundary line between their two small backyards and had been a favorite spot for years—it was here that he'd told her, just after moving to town, that his parents were divorced, here that she'd confessed her seventh-grade terror of having no friends, here that, at twelve, they'd shared their first kiss. It was where they ran to when they needed to run away, where their most terrible secrets lived. It was their place, the only thing in the world they truly owned—and they owned it together.

But they hadn't needed their rock in a long time.

"Well, what do you want to do?" she asked simply.

"That's all you're going to say?" He rubbed his eyes furiously, like a little boy trying to rub out his tears. "Don't you want to tell me what a disgusting pig I am, or something?"

"I think I'll let Beth have that honor, if she ever finds out." And Harper almost immediately began sifting through her options—maybe she could play this to her advantage after all. If she could find the right angle, if little Bethie heard the news in just the right way . . .

"Oh God," Adam gasped, his voice filled with horror. "Do you think she will? What am I saying, of course she will. And then . . ."

"Adam, chill out," Harper advised, trying to keep her voice steady. "She probably won't find out—I'm obviously not going to tell her, Kaia has no reason to tell her—and I assume *you're* not going to tell her?"

Though the spineless brat would probably take about five seconds to forgive you, Harper thought with disgust.

"God, no. Unless—should I? Harper, I'm so screwed up. I don't know what I'm doing."

"So, like I said, what do you *want* to do?" Harper repeated. "Ball's in your court, Ad."

She shivered. It was a cold night, a brisk wind blowing

through the yard, and she was dressed in only cords and a lacy tank top. Before she could even say anything—not that she would have said anything, nothing could have forced her to interrupt *this* train of thought—Adam pulled off his sweatshirt and tossed it to her. Beneath it, she noticed, he was wearing a vintage Transformers T-shirt she'd bought him for his birthday last year.

"What I want?" he mused, as Harper zipped herself into the cozy red fleece. "I want to go back to the beginning of the year and start over, do everything different."

"Not an option," she pointed out. "Try again."

He was silent for a moment, and Harper wondered whether it was time for her to take a harder line. If he didn't know what he wanted, well, maybe she should just enlighten him.

"Remember when I kissed you out here?" he asked suddenly.

"Barely," she said casually, hoping he couldn't hear the heartbeat pounding in her ears. "Our braces got stuck together and you accidentally stuck your tongue up my nose—but other than that, it was a success."

They laughed quietly together.

"Everything was easier then," Adam finally said softly, his voice almost carried away on the wind. "I miss it—you and me, just having fun, being together."

"We hated it," Harper reminded him. "We were bored out of our minds. We just wanted to grow up."

Adam sighed. "Yeah, and look where that got us."

Harper watched his silhouette in the moonlight and then, because it felt right, and because she wasn't scared anymore, she took his hand. His fingers curled around hers, and she squeezed his hand gently. He gave her a quick squeeze back. They lay together on the rock, side by side, connected. She hadn't felt so close to him in a long time. This was it. This was her moment.

"Adam, maybe—maybe it's not supposed to be so hard," she suggested hesitantly. "Maybe being with Beth should be *easy*. Maybe if it's not—well, maybe you don't really want to be with her. Maybe you want—"

He pulled his hand away from hers and sat up.

"That's not what I was saying at all, Harper," he said hotly. But the sudden anger, the quick retort—maybe, Harper realized, he knew she was right. "I *love* her," he insisted. "It's not supposed to be easy."

"I know . . . but this?" she pushed. "Fighting all the time? Sleeping with someone else? You have to admit—it doesn't really sound like a good, healthy relationship."

"So we're going through a bad time," he protested—and from the look on his face, she wondered if she'd gone a step too far. "You don't just walk away when things are tough."

"Adam, I just—"

"Or maybe that's what *you* do," he said scornfully, leaping off the rock. "And maybe that's why you're always alone. You're so used to being alone, I don't even think you realize it—but maybe if you did, you wouldn't even care." He turned his back on her and walked inside.

Harper lay on the rock, perfectly still, watching the stars and listening to the silence of the night. She pulled Adam's sweatshirt tightly around her and breathed in the smell of him, still lingering on the soft fleece.

She did know, better than anyone. And she cared.

There are times when a girl just needs to be alone.

This was not one of them.

Harper hit the speed dial and waited impatiently for Miranda to pick up the phone. Finally, on the fourth ring, just when she'd almost given up hope, salvation arrived.

"911, Miranda," she said, by way of greeting. "This is an emergency situation. We're going out."

"Harper, I've got a test tomorrow, I've got to study, I—"

Harper wasn't listening. She was too busy digging through her closet, searching. She needed the perfect outfit for a feel-good, look-better night on the town. And there it was. Spangled tube top—green, to match her eyes; skintight miniskirt—black, to match her mood. The strappy silver stiletto heels she never got the chance to wear. And a black beaded choker, to dress her naked neck. She pulled her hair back into a loose, low chignon, making sure that a few curly tendrils hung down over her eyes. It was a definite look. A little sweet, a little sassy; slightly slutty, but not too skanky. Basically—hot. Maybe a little out of place in the low-rent nightlife options Grace provided her, but if she got whistled at by some drunken trucker or hit on by a Hell's Angel, well, so much the better. It would be a reminder that plenty of people out there wanted her—more than half the high school, for one (99 percent of the male half, with a few alterna-females thrown in for good measure, or so she'd been told). And tonight, she could use all the reminders she could get.

Miranda was still babbling on about a test, and some bio lab that needed to be written up.

"Miranda, listen to me," Harper cut in impatiently.

"SOS. Seriously, drop what you're doing—we're going out."

It took some persuading, some wheedling, and eventually a promise from Harper that she would treat Miranda to a manicure in time for the formal that weekend and would finish burning all the CDs for the after party on her own. Still, Miranda hedged—it was late, she was tired, she was in her pajamas, her parents would be suspicious. . . .

But Harper was nothing if not persistent—and Miranda was nothing if not loyal, and so, finally, she hung up the phone and answered the call.

As far as their parents were concerned, Harper was sleeping at Miranda's house and Miranda was sleeping at Harper's. All thanks to a supposed late-night cram session for an imaginary chem test. (Harper's parents foolishly thought that Miranda was a good influence, and as far as Miranda's mother was concerned, Harper was the golden child. It was almost too easy.) Later they'd sneak into Harper's house to get some sleep, knowing that her parents, always up and out by five a.m., would never know they'd been there.

As for the night's *real* entertainment, they settled on the Barnstormer, a seedy ribs joint on the north side of town that attracted a reliable clientele of truckers, motorcyclists, and a few regulars, who, by the time they passed through the red wooden doors, were already too drunk to pass along any information about their station in life (or possibly even to remember it themselves).

It was dark, smoky, and crowded, the perfect place to lose yourself and your problems. A sober observer would have spotted Harper and Miranda immediately—the two young girls, dressed to kill, were several decades younger and several layers of dirt cleaner than the majority of patrons. But by eleven p.m. on Rodeo Night, the only sober observers available were the waitresses, who, spending most of their time fending off wandering hands and cleaning up patches of vomit, had little inclination to bother the two girls from the slightly less wrong side of the tracks.

Feeling cloaked by a powerful haze of invisibility, they grabbed a small table in the dark recesses of the bar and, carefully avoiding any sticky spots, flagged down a waitress. Their order:

Two baskets of chicken wings.

One basket of ribs.

Two pitchers of beer.

It was going to be that kind of night.

As the twangs of country-and-western music blared in the background, Harper and Miranda spilled out their problems to each other, becoming increasingly incoherent and increasingly convinced that their problems could be easily solved by the elimination of all men from the face of the Earth. But, it seemed, nothing short of that would help.

A few years ago, the owner of the Barnstormer—a quietly practical middle-aged woman who had moved to Grace after the sudden death of her husband and concluded that the only money to be found in a town like this was in providing its population with food, drinks, or women (she'd hit the trifecta)—had hung a large piece of driftwood over the inside entrance. The red paint scrawled across it offered a legend to all who passed beneath: EAT TILL IT HURTS, DRINK TILL IT FEELS BETTER.

By midnight Harper and Miranda had done both.

Long years of practice had taught Harper and Miranda that the quickest way to feel better was to remind themselves that other people were so much worse. And Rodeo Night at the Barnstormer provided them plenty of opportunity.

"Check out the guy in the cowboy boots," Miranda crowed, almost spitting out her mouthful of beer.

"Which one?" Harper asked, rolling her eyes. "They're *all* wearing cowboy boots."

"Yeah, but most of them are wearing a little bit more than that," Miranda pointed out, nodding her head to the right, where an overweight, middle-aged guy had stripped off his shirt and climbed atop the bar, gyrating and bouncing in time to the Garth Brooks jukebox beat and the hoots of the crowd.

They dissolved into laughter. This town was filled with enough losers to cheer them up well into the next decade.

"How about the Lone Ranger over there?" Harper snorted, pointing in the direction of an old man decked out in a fifties cowboy costume, complete with mask and capgun.

"God, we have got to get out of this town before we turn into one of them," Miranda declared. She grabbed the last barbecue wing and stuffed it into her mouth, then downed the rest of her beer.

"Tell me about it," Harper agreed, finishing her own. They poured themselves more from the pitcher and sloppily toasted, clinking their overflowing glasses.

"To us!" Miranda crowed.

"To getting the hell out of this place!" Harper added.

"To living fabulous lives—"

"Without shitty guys dragging us down!"

"To being wild and crazy—"

"And independent, on our own—"

"Together!" Miranda finished triumphantly.

And they drank up.

Beth had stayed home from school that day. She'd told her mother she was sick, and her mother had no reason not to believe her. For why would Bethie lie?

She'd spent the day in bed, and it was almost as if she were sick—she was immobilized. Normally unable to sit still for more than a few minutes at a time, her mind always on fire thinking of the next task to be done, the next mission to accomplish, she'd spent the day tucked neatly under her covers staring aimlessly at the TV and flipping between channels.

Talk show.

Soap opera.

Dora the Explorer.

Soap opera.

It was all the same to her.

She knew she couldn't hide in her room forever, battering herself with accusations and regrets, if only's and what if's.

If only I hadn't gone to the meeting.

If only I hadn't flirted with him.

If only I'd known what he wanted from me.

What if I wanted it too?

She'd have to leave her sanctuary someday. She'd have to face her life, face him, and soon.

Just not today.

There was a knock on her door.

"Beth? Honey?" Without waiting for Beth to respond, her mother opened the door a few inches and poked her head through the gap. "How are you feeling, sweetheart?" Her face was filled with concern, and Beth felt a momentary stab of guilt for lying, but beneath that, a warm glow of pleasure—her mother was usually too busy to remember that Beth existed, much less worry about how she was doing. In fact, Beth realized, this was the first time in months that her mother had even set foot inside her room.

"I'm okay, I guess," she said listlessly, not bothering to look away from the TV.

"Are you feeling up for a visitor?" her mother asked, glancing over her shoulder into the hallway.

Beth sat up in bed and looked over at the clock. It was almost eleven—who would be visiting her? Usually she wasn't even allowed to have guests in the house this late— her parents were afraid it would wake up the twins.

"I know it's late," her mother added, "but he says he brought you your homework, so I thought just this once it would be okay."

He?

Beth nodded weakly, and her mother swung open the door all the way—revealing Adam, standing in the hallway with his hands behind his back and an adorable smile on his face.

As her mother disappeared and Adam came into the room, Beth panicked briefly, running her hands through her tangled hair and looking down at her ragged pajamas— she'd been in bed all day, hadn't brushed her teeth in hours or brushed her hair since yesterday. She was a total mess, and for a second, she was tempted to hide under the covers until he went away, but then he came and sat down on the bed next to her and all she could think was: He came. For me.

"Claire already called to give me all the homework," she told him—and then realized that she hadn't even thanked him for coming. She'd only just gotten him back, and now, if her scarecrow appearance didn't send him screaming in the other direction, her rudeness probably would.

"I know she did," he said, before she could say anything else.

"Then why—?"

"I wanted to give you something," he told her, brushing a lock of hair off her forehead. "Well, two things, actually. First, this."

He leaned down and kissed her softly on the lips—and if her parents hadn't been on the other side of the paperthin walls, Beth would have been tempted to wrap her arms around him and throw him down onto the bed beside her. But instead, she just kissed him back gently, breathing deeply. He tasted like cinnamon, and she knew it was probably because he'd just finished a pack of the cinnamon-flavored gum he was addicted to. And she loved that she knew things like that about him. No matter how bad things got, she still knew him. And he knew her, better than anyone else.

"That's not all," he said, pulling away. She wrapped her fingers through his, and he squeezed her hand gently, and with his other hand unzipped his backpack, pulled something out, and presented it to her.

It was a red rose, beautiful and perfect. And it was threaded through a pink plastic flower ring—an exact match to the one he'd given her so long ago, just before their first date.

Beth laughed, and it felt like the first time she'd laughed in years.

"I'm still not marrying you, idiot," she giggled. But she took the giant ring and slipped it onto her finger.

"I thought we'd start slow," he said, just as he had all those months ago. "One date."

"What are you talking about?" she asked, inhaling the sweet fragrance of the rose. It was almost overpowering.

"Come to the formal with me," he asked.

Beth shook her head in confusion. "I'm already going with you," she reminded him. "You asked me weeks ago." She'd been saving up to buy a new dress, actually, but then they'd been fighting so much and had stopped speaking and eventually wasting all that money on a dress she might not get to wear hadn't seemed like such a great idea. But now, looking into his earnest blue eyes, now she couldn't think of anything she wanted to do more than look beautiful for him. To turn back time and forget about everything that had happened this month—*everything*. This weekend, this dance, it would be just the fresh start they needed.

"A lot's happened since then," Adam explained. "I've been an asshole since then," he added.

"No, it wasn't you, it was just—"

"Let me finish," he interrupted quietly. "I've been a jerk, and now I know it, and I just want us to start over again, fresh. Just pretend the last few weeks never happened. So, Ms. Manning, will you do me the great honor of going to the dance with me?" He pulled the rose from her fingers and played its petals gently across her lips.

"Well, I'll have to think about it for a second," she began with a frown. His face crumpled, and she rewarded him with a bright grin. "Of course I'll go with you." She moved the rose out of the way and put her arms around him, cradling his face in her hands. She pulled his face toward her and kissed him, wishing that she could freeze this moment, that they really could pretend that the last few weeks had never happened and that the future would never come. That there would be no more arguments, that the tension that crackled between them would just disappear and things would be sweet and easy again, like they were tonight. And, she realized, she knew how to make that happen.

"I love you, Adam," she whispered, her lips still just barely touching his.

"You too, Beth. Only you."

And even though it was late and her mother could burst into the room at any minute, Beth kissed him again. The moment couldn't last forever—but she wasn't ready to let it end.

chapter

15

Miranda wasn't fat.

She knew that much, at least.

After all, she wasn't *crazy*, she told herself, looking in the mirror. No double chins or rolls of fat—she certainly wasn't one of those girls who looked like a skeleton but imagined a blimp. She knew what she saw.

And what she saw wasn't much.

Short—an inch above freakish but only barely within the "cute" zone. Dull reddish hair. Pale, washed-out skin. Thick ankles (which she hadn't even noticed until her mother had oh-so-kindly pointed them out to her and helpfully suggested she steer clear of skirts). Bulky thighs. Somehow, sometime, the lithe, slim body she'd had when she was younger—the one she'd never noticed until one of her mother's friends commented in envious awe on how she could "eat like an elephant and look like a giraffe"—had disappeared.

Now, she was just—medium. Bland. She knew that

under other circumstances, in other, bigger towns, she wouldn't be best friends with the school's alpha girl; the A list wouldn't notice her.

But in this life, in this town, she was best friends with Harper—which is why she'd gone along with the drunken suggestion that they ditch their dates for the stupid formal and go on their own. Prove to the world that they didn't need guys, that they'd have more fun without some testosterone-charged idiots pawing at them all night.

She twirled once more in front of the mirror, her gauzy black dress flaring out as she spun.

The other night at the Barnstormer, filled with alcoholic courage, spending the dance on the sidelines with Harper, watching a roomful of glamorous, dewy-eyed couples spin around the auditorium had sounded perfect.

Funny—in the sober light of day (or rather, in the sober half-light of twilight, awaiting her ride)—it was starting to sound slightly less than perfect. Asinine. Insane. Pretty much the worst idea she'd ever heard.

But unless she wanted to take her father as a date, it was too late to do anything about it. She ran a brush through her hair one last time and quickly put on another layer of lip gloss. Her ride wasn't due for another twenty minutes, but she was done getting ready. Her parents—who had no idea there even *was* a dance—were out for the night. Miranda hadn't wanted to suffer through them fawning all over her, pinching her cheeks and taking pictures—or even worse, suffer through them ignoring the whole thing and going out anyway. Better not to risk it. So the house was empty, she had plenty of time to kill—and there was a bottle of gin in the cabinet next to the sink that had her name on it.

She had a feeling she was going to need it.

When Kane had suggested that she and Miranda ride over to the dance with him, he hadn't mentioned anything about the car—a limo. Sort of. It had a big backseat, all right, and a chauffeur up front, just like a real limo—but that was where the similarities ended. Kane's chariot of choice was a garish pink 1960s convertible, roughly the size of a boat, that made Harper feel like she was riding around inside a giant bottle of Pepto-Bismol. He also hadn't mentioned anything about his date. And that, as it turned out, was a much bigger problem.

"What are *you* doing here?" Harper sneered as she climbed into the car and took a seat—right across from Kaia.

"Nice manners," Kane chided her. "Didn't I mention it the other day? Kaia's my date." He slung an arm around the ice queen, who was draped in a shimmery Anna Sui gown the color of emeralds. Even Harper had to admit that it was stunning—though not out loud.

"Whatever, let's just get going and pick up Miranda," she snapped. "We're late."

"Aren't you going to say anything about our ride?" Kane asked. He gestured around the spacious backseat of the vintage convertible. "Limos are so—junior high prom. At least this has some style."

"What do I think?" Harper mused, glancing disdain-fully at the velour seats—hot pink to match the exterior. She raised a hand to her hair, which had been carefully smoothed back into an elaborate upsweep—thanks to the lack of a roof on the rose monstrosity, she'd probably arrive at the dance looking like she had a bird's nest on top of her head. "I think I like your taste in cars about as much as I like your taste in women."

"Classy, Harper, real classy," Kane told her scornfully. Kaia, who had yet to say a word, just smiled and slid a hand onto Kane's inner thigh. She leaned over and, eyes never leaving Harper's face, whispered something in his ear.

Kane's eyes widened, and they both laughed.

"My thoughts exactly," he said, and began kissing her neck. As his hand grazed Kaia's breast and her lips found his, Harper recoiled in disgust.

Classy, Kane, real classy, she thought. It was going to be a long night.

Adam always looked handsome in a tux. With his broad chest and chiseled features, he looked like a film star from the fifties, full of glamour and chivalry, ready to sweep her away on some elegant adventure. He gently pinned on a small corsage—a delicate white rose—and she wondered how her eye ever could have strayed to someone else. Much less a teacher.

All the stupid fighting—she'd come so close to losing him. Beth shivered at the thought.

"Are you cold?" he asked, tucking her silver wrap around her shoulders and rubbing his warm hand up and down her back.

Inside the house everything had been so loud. Her brothers running circles around them. Her parents hopping up and down, snapping pictures and fawning over Beth as if they'd never seen her in a dress before. But out here on her front step, it was quiet and dark. Just the two of them.

"I'm fine," she assured him. "Let's get going." She was eager to get to the dance—and through the dance—because she had a surprise waiting for Adam at the end of the night. The sooner it came, the less time she'd have to worry about it.

She'd never ridden in a limousine before, and when she saw the long black car waiting outside her tiny house, she stopped and closed her eyes, savoring the moment. Then Adam took her hand and they walked down the path together to the curb, where their carriage awaited. It was such a romantic, regal procession, under such a bright, starry sky.

Beth felt like a princess—and she knew it was going to be a perfect night.

"Have I told you how beautiful you look tonight?" Adam asked, handing her a glass of champagne and leaning back against the seat of the limo. It had set him back a hundred bucks, but it was worth it for the look on Beth's face. He owed her so much—she could never know how much.

"Only a couple hundred times or so," Beth laughed, tucking a tendril of hair behind her ears and blushing. "But keep going, please."

"Ravishingly beautiful. Awe-inspiringly beautiful," he told her, moving closer. "The most beautiful thing I've ever seen. More beautiful than—"

She kissed him, and he drank in the intoxicating feel of her.

It wasn't just a line. She really was more beautiful than

he'd ever seen her—the pale blue of her dress matched the deep ocean of her eyes, and its silky material hugged her body, revealing curves that he hadn't even realized she had. Her cornflower blond hair, usually loose and flowing over her shoulders, was swept up into a loose bun, long tendrils framing her delicate face. And the way she was smiling—it was radiant, almost mysterious, as if she had some secret happy thought hidden away in the recesses of her mind. She was glowing—and looking at him as if he was the one who'd made her glow. Even the way she held her glass, her long, slender fingers curling around the narrow stem— even that was soft, elegant, perfect.

She was perfect. And every time she looked at him with her loving, trusting eyes, he had to look away in shame. After all, every word out of his mouth was a lie, just pretty phrases designed to hide the truth. He could mean them all he wanted—and he did—but it wouldn't change things. It wouldn't change the one thing he could never say.

"Are you okay, Ad?" she asked, and he realized he'd been staring at her.

He smiled.

"Just thinking of what a great night we're going to have together," he told her. Another lie.

More lies piled up by the minute, and his skin crawled with the fear that everything was going to come apart. Especially tonight—when he and Kaia, and worse, Beth and Kaia, were bound to come face-to-face.

"It's going to be a wonderful night," Beth sighed, leaning her head on his shoulder. "It's going to be perfect."

Adam slugged back his glass of champagne and poured himself another—anything to get him through the night.

Perfect?

Unlikely.

Miranda jumped out of the car almost before it pulled to a full stop—it had been all she could do to restrain herself from jumping out miles ago, at full speed. Between Harper and Kaia's intermittent sniping and Kane and Kaia's apparent inability to keep their hands off each other, the fifteen-minute ride had felt like an eternity.

Now that they were finally here, she just wanted to get out and away as quickly as possible—and if she managed to avoid being seen emerging from Kane's hot pink cotton candy machine, that would also be a perk. Though the way her luck was running, it seemed unlikely. Speaking of incognito—

"Harper!" It was Harper's hideously annoying sophomore clone.

"Miranda!" And her equally annoying sidekick.

"Kane and Kaia!" they chorused. "Hiiiii!"

It was too late to escape. The two girls, dressed in identical satin slip dresses (Mini-Me in lavender, Mini-She in eggshell blue) tottered up to them on shaky heels. Their dates, two pimply sophomores who, in matching crew cuts and rented tuxedos, looked as identical to each other as the Minis (one was blond, one was brunette—they were otherwise interchangeable), trudged dutifully behind them.

Kaia, Harper, and Miranda each nodded wearily at the fan club—Kane couldn't even be bothered to do that much.

"Kaia, your dress is gorgeous," Mini-Me gushed. "Where'd you get it?"

"Bitches-R-Us?" Harper suggested.

"Anna Sui, actually." Kaia glared at Harper. "Where'd you get yours, Wal-Mart?"

"That's where I got mine, too!" Mini-She cried. She linked arms with Harper and leaned toward her conspiratorially. "So, Harper," she asked in a low voice, "where's your date?"

"Oh, Harper and Miranda came together," Kaia simpered. "Isn't that adorable?"

Now it was Harper's turn to glare. She extricated herself from the sophomore and moved quickly over to Miranda's side.

"Are you guys, like, a couple now?" Mini-Me asked, eyes agog.

"No, no," Miranda said hastily. God, this was just what she'd been afraid of. Worse, even. "We're just—I—"

"We told our dates to go screw themselves," Harper jumped in. She glanced at Kaia. "Not *everyone's* self-esteem is dependent on testosterone."

"Looking for some testosterone?" Kane asked, suddenly paying attention. "Why didn't you say so?"

He grabbed Kaia and swooped her down into a dramatic dip, kissing her as her hair grazed the ground. The sophomores giggled and Harper and Miranda just shook their heads until finally he pulled her up and took her hand.

"Well, milady, shall we away?"

And they walked inside, Mini-Me, Mini-She, and their unfortunate dates in hot pursuit.

"Suck it up, Rand," Harper said, as Miranda's eyes followed Kane's figure into the gym. "You know he could care less about her—he's just trying to be an asshole."

"He's doing a pretty good job of it," Miranda admitted.

"Now see, that's what I've been trying to tell you," Harper pointed out. She grabbed Miranda's arm and pulled her forward. "Come on, let's go find some real men. You ready for this?"

Miranda nodded and followed silently. *Here we go,* she thought gloomily. *Ready—or not.*

chapter

16

The high school gym had been transformed. A diligent team of party planners (culled from a joint task force of student council members, cheerleaders, and some devoted PTA moms) had hung enough multicolored leaves, paper lanterns, and "welcome back" banners to turn the place into an autumnal paradise. Could you even tell that beneath all those decorations lay a dirty, smelly, multipurpose room that, in two days, would once again be filled with sweaty students and the occasional fistfight?

In a minute.

It even smelled the same, Adam mused, looking around in disdain at the tacky setup. He supposed all this crap was some girl's idea of romantic—he was just glad it wasn't anyone he had to date.

"Is her back turned?" Kane asked Adam, who was supposed to be on the lookout for the nearest chaperone. They stood in a back corner, just under the bleachers—

the exact spot that, if the teachers had any sense at all, they'd be watching around the clock. Where else would you go to make trouble? Fortunately for would-be troublemakers, common sense was commonly absent among the Haven High faculty—or at least, those unsavvy enough to get themselves roped into chaperoning a school dance.

"Yeah, you're clear," Adam assured him. "Not that she'd see you." (Dolores Martin, the school librarian, was about 140 years old and hadn't been able to see more than ten feet ahead of her since the Nixon administration.) "What are you up to, anyway?"

"I told you, it's a surprise," Kane said mysteriously. "I've equipped everyone else, but I had to improvise." He pointed toward one of the guys from the swim team, who was gulping from a plastic bottle.

"Vitamin water?" Adam asked, peering at the bottle.

"Yeah, new flavor—kiwi strawberry with a little something extra."

"Extra?"

"Vodka can be very healthy for you, you know," Kane confided with a laugh. "But for you, my friend, something special. A little more risk—but a lot more style." He pulled a tiny silver flask from inside his jacket and surreptitiously passed it to Adam. "Just don't get caught."

Adam fumbled the flask for a moment, then pushed it back toward Kane. He could see it now—the laser beam eyes of his AP history teacher spotting a glint of silver coming out of his pocket. Getting pulled out of Beth's arms and hauled off the dance floor in front of everyone. Thrown out, disgraced. Beth would certainly never forgive him for ruining her night over something so stupid. No, he had enough to worry about already.

"Doesn't seem like a great idea," Adam explained, as Kane shook his head and slipped the flask into one of his outer pockets. "Especially the way my luck is going. Last thing I need is to get suspended for getting drunk on school property or something."

"Your call," Kane said ruefully. "Well, I guess a man in love doesn't need any other forms of intoxication. Speaking of which, I better go collect my date before your beloved tells her too many lies about me. Or worse"—he raised his eyebrows—"the truth."

Adam followed Kane's gaze across the room and, with alarm, saw Beth and Kaia in a corner, deep in conversation.

His heart missed a couple of hundred beats.

"Uh, you're right, we better go break that up," he stammered. Kane started off, but Adam grabbed him and pulled him back.

"Changed my mind," he whispered, slipping the flask out of Kane's pocket and, checking to make sure no one was watching, downing half its contents.

He felt better already.

"So what did you need to tell me?" Beth asked impatiently, glancing across the room at Adam. She held back a smile as she thought about what they'd be doing later tonight. If he only knew. She just wanted to be with him—and away from Kaia, who'd pinned her in a corner for some mysteriously urgent reason that had evaporated as soon as she'd gotten Beth alone.

"Have I told you how great you look tonight?" Kaia asked sweetly.

"Thanks. Can you just tell me what was so important?" The DJ had just started a slow song. "Take My Breath Away"—a little cheesy, maybe, but one of Beth's favorites. She wanted to be swaying back and forth to the melody, eyes closed, head on Adam's shoulder. Not here.

"What? Oh, that was nothing. I mean, I thought you might want to know that Adam—" Kaia cut herself off with a sigh. "Oh . . . Check out Mr. Powell—doesn't he look hot tonight in his tux?"

"What about Adam?" Beth persisted. The last thing she wanted to think about was Jack Powell, or how good he looked in his tux. Which, despite her best efforts, she'd already noticed.

"Oh, we can finish this later. Maybe you want to go talk to Mr. Powell?" Kaia asked innocently. "I won't mind—I know how *close* you two are."

For the moment Beth forgot about Adam and whatever secret was about to be revealed and studied Kaia closely. Did she—could she possibly—know?

"We're not close," she said coolly, deciding, or at least desperately hoping, that Kaia didn't know what she was saying. "And if you ask me, he's not a very good teacher. Working with him on the newspaper sucks."

"That's not what I heard," Kaia said with a sly grin.

"What are you talking about?" Beth asked in a hushed voice. All her breath had slipped away.

But before Kaia could answer, Kane snuck up behind her and grabbed her waist, twirling her around. A moment later, Beth felt Adam's strong hands around her as he lifted her off the ground and swung her into his arms. She hoped he couldn't feel her trembling.

"So what's going on over here?" Kane asked, once the girls had stopped squealing.

"Trust me," Kaia said, looking directly at Adam. "You don't want to know."

Lucky break that Powell was chaperoning the dance.

Luckier still that he was standing amidst a small circle of other teachers. Kaia knew that no self-respecting chaperone could turn down an innocent request to dance with one of his students—at least, not without having a lot of explaining to do.

Kaia excused herself and strode over to the cluster of teachers. Powell, seeing her approach, was already preparing his getaway.

"Mr. Powell!" she exclaimed. "You look so handsome in your tuxedo! Think you could spare me a dance?"

He glared at her, then smiled for the sake of the group.

"Oh, Kaia, I'm not much of a dancer—you know, two left feet and all."

"Go for it, Jack," urged Mr. Holcomb, from the English department.

"Yes, 'cut a rug,'" the librarian added.

The group began to laugh as Kaia led a reluctant Mr. Powell onto the floor. She knew what they were thinking: *How adorable, a little crush.* Well, let them think what they wanted—she knew what she was doing.

Kaia looped her arms around his neck and his hands found a spot on her waist—he held her rigidly, carefully keeping a half foot of space between them.

"Did I not make myself clear before, Ms. Sellers?" The amiable facade was gone. Good. "You and me? It's never going to happen. And certainly not in the middle of a crowded dance floor with the whole school looking on."

"Oh, I know, Mr. Powell," she said, lowering her eyes and giving him an exaggeratedly chastened look. "After all, it's your policy not to mix business with pleasure, right?"

"I don't consort with students, yes, if that's what you mean," he said stiffly.

"And I don't consort with *liars*," Kaia hissed.

He stopped dancing and pushed her away.

"What's that supposed to mean?" But some of the steely certainty had faded from his voice.

She put her arms around him again.

"Better keep dancing, and keep smiling, Mr. Powell— you don't want your friends over there thinking we're having a lovers' spat." She gave a friendly wave to the group of teachers smiling and cheering them on from the sidelines.

"I'll ask you again, what are you talking about?" he repeated, smiling through gritted teeth.

"I'm talking about your nonexistent policy, Mr. Powell. I'm talking about your loose relationship with the truth and your looser one with the rules." She moved in closer and lowered her voice to a whisper. "I'm talking about you and Beth—I *saw* you."

"I'm quite sure I don't know what you mean," Powell protested. His face had gone white. "There was nothing to see."

"Right," Kaia said sarcastically. "I hope that's not the poker face you're planning to use when you talk to the principal, or the school board, or hey, the police—"

His fingers tightened on her waist.

"That's right, the police," Kaia said. "Small town like this, full of all those family values, I imagine they don't look too kindly on this sort of thing. Teacher preying on innocent students. We're just children, really. . . ."

"You don't want to screw with me, Kaia," he warned her in a low, ominous voice.

"Not anymore," she said lightly, shaking her head. "No, you chose someone else for that—and I can live with it. I just hope that *you* can."

And, waving again in the direction of Powell's fellow teachers, she squeezed in close to Jack Powell and slammed her lips to his, jamming her tongue into his mouth before he knew what was happening, and then, with a less than gentle nibble on his lip, she pushed him away.

"See you around, Mr. Powell—you can count on it."

Beth, Adam, Miranda, and Harper witnessed the scene from the sidelines with a mixture of shock, awe, and horror (in different proportions, depending on the witness).

"That girl is unbelievable," Harper gasped. "What the hell is she thinking?"

"Unbelievable is right," Adam repeated, sounding almost impressed. Beth looked at him sharply, and his eyes shot down to the ground, avoiding her gaze. In his pocket, his hand tightened around the now empty flask.

"Bet you wish you had the nerve to do that, Beth," Miranda laughed. "I know I do."

Beth stammered and blushed and mumbled something about nothing, and finally Harper cut in.

"Oh, please, Beth's not that pathetic, and neither are you, Miranda. She practically jumped down his throat—it was embarrassing to watch! What was that you were saying about her being so sad and misunderstood, Adam?"

Now it was Adam's turn to stammer nonsensically.

"It's really, uh, none of our business," he finally said, turning away from the dance floor, where Mr. Powell was still standing alone and motionless, only barely visible through the swirling wall of dancers.

"You're totally right," Beth added with relief. "Let's just dance."

"Definitely." He clasped her by the hand and led her quickly onto the dance floor, leaving Harper and Miranda behind in disbelief.

"None of our business?" Miranda asked. "Since when does that stop us? Is this a new policy I wasn't told about?"

"I guess we both missed the memo," Harper said in disgust. "Look at them." She gestured weakly toward Beth and Adam, who were slowly swaying in each other's arms, despite the fast-paced rock song blaring through the speakers. "He can't keep his hands off her for a minute."

"This dance sucks," Miranda said.

"Tell me about it."

They stood together at the edge of the action, watching dozens of couples swirling around the floor. That was the problem with scoping for hot guys at school formals. The inspirational girl-power-themed episodes of bad TV shows notwithstanding, the fact was that all the normal guys showed up to these things with dates. So unless you were ready to break up a matched pair and leave some unfortunate girl drying the tearstains on her dress under the bathroom hand blower (not that Harper hadn't left her share of those in her wake), you were shit out of luck. No, instead you were stuck with prizes like Lester Lawrence, decked out in a sky blue tux and ruffled Hawaiian shirt, and his gang of losers. Miranda was sure any one of them would be happy to dance with her. Great.

And then, like Prince Charming, appearing as if by magic out of the mist: Kane.

He strode purposefully toward them, with Kaia nowhere in sight.

"You ladies look bored," he said. "How about a dance?"

For a moment Miranda, who figured any drugs harder than pot weren't worth the dead brain cells, finally understood what people were always talking about, that rush of ecstasy, a shot of pure joy exploding out of you, so powerful that it shut out the world for a moment, threatened to sweep you away.

But it was just for a moment.

Because when she came down to earth, Kane's words still ringing in her ears (familiar words, as he'd uttered them so often in the G-rated portion of her fantasies), she realized that his arm was outstretched to Harper. Of course.

Harper took his hand and headed toward the dance floor, shooting Miranda an apologetic look over her shoulder. There was nothing to apologize for, of course. This was just the way it worked.

Couples danced, the band played, Lester Lawrence talked to the pet grasshopper in his pocket, and Miranda stood on the fringes of it all.

Alone.

That's life, right? *C'est la vie.*

Kane swung her around the dance floor, moving effortlessly in time with the music, now a slow R&B groove. He danced with ease, skill, and grace—the same way he did everything else. (If Kane couldn't do it well, he didn't do it at all.)

"Having a good time, Grace?" he asked.

"Not particularly." There was no point in putting on a brave face, since she was sure he couldn't care less. "How about you? Enjoying your date with our very own Lolita?" She spotted Kaia on the sidelines, fending off a crowd of curiosity seekers—Mini-Me, she was pleased to see, among them. Harper supposed she should be a bit dismayed that her own personal fan club seemed to be redevoting itself to Kaia-worship, as it was just another sign of the rich bitch encroaching on her territory. But somehow, she just couldn't work up the energy—besides, having the sophomore squad chase after her was, in the end, far more punishment than reward.

"I'm enjoying myself very much, thanks," Kane replied. "Of course, not as much as *him*." He swung her around, bringing her face-to-face with Adam and Beth, arms draped loosely around each other, swaying in the middle of the dance floor, clearly in a world of their own. Their eyes were closed, and Beth's head rested on Adam's broad shoulder. He ran his hands slowly up and down her back.

Harper felt sick. She looked away—right into Kane's disgustingly knowing grin.

"Jealous?"

Harper said nothing.

"Just letting you know, my offer still stands. You and me, the anti-Cupids. Just say the word."

Harper stole another glance at the happy couple. Adam was now running his fingers through her long, blond hair.

God, it was tempting.

"Mind if I cut in?"

Harper breathed a sigh of relief—Kaia's icy voice had never been more welcome. "He is *my* date, after all," Kaia pointed out snottily.

Harper let her hands drop and stepped away.

"My pleasure—he's all yours." She walked away—but not quickly enough that she didn't overhear Kaia's parting shot.

"It's so sweet of you to keep Harper company, Kane," she oozed. "You know, since she couldn't find a date of her own."

Harper resisted the temptation to turn back and slap her—and the marginally more powerful temptation to take another look (or extended, longing stare) at Adam. Instead she kept her eyes focused on Miranda, lingering next to a large bowl of pretzels and looking forlorn; she focused on Miranda and, about ten feet behind her, the exit.

It was time to get the hell out.

When the going gets tough, the tough get stoned. Which is exactly what Harper and Miranda proceeded to do.

They stopped off at the after party (Harper: "After all, we planned the damn thing") but after ascertaining that all the details were in place—beer, music, lanterns, illicit acts featuring Haven High's elite—they ditched out. (Harper: "Just a bunch of losers getting laid.") Kane had roped scuzzy Reed Sawyer into supervising things so that the rest of them could focus on their night of debauchery—all it took was a dime bag of weed and a six-pack; apparently Reed didn't have anything better to do anyway. A burnout like him certainly wouldn't be caught dead at a school dance—and there was no way he would have made it onto the invite list under any other circumstances, but Harper supposed that climbing his way up the Haven High social ladder wasn't too high on his list of priorities. *Getting* high? Yes. Scoring some kind of record deal for his posse of talentless losers? Probably. But that was about it. Trust Kane to find a guy like that.

He lay sprawled on one of the motel's musty sofas and lazily watched the chaos swirl around him. Harper wasn't sure exactly what "supervising" was supposed to entail—yes, he'd turned on the music and made sure that the kegs were tapped and flowing, but if someone tried to make off with the stereo or burn the place down, would this guy be willing or able to do anything about it? Harper highly doubted it—but at the moment, she didn't really care.

Besides, back at Miranda's place, the parents were out, the pot was ample, the beer didn't come from a keg, and there were no unidentifiable fluids or condom packages littering the floor. Nor was there anyone they didn't want to talk to—which, at the moment, included pretty much everyone except for each other.

It took an hour for the one taxi company in town to dispatch a driver—but it was well worth the wait. (It was also worth it not to have to ride away from the party in the hot pink monstrosity that had carried them to the dance.)

"Did you see Lauren's dress?" Miranda asked once they were safely ensconced in her bedroom. She exhaled a puff of smoke and flopped back onto her bed.

"How could I miss it? It was practically fluorescent!" Harper cackled, taking the joint from Miranda and inhaling deeply. She was sitting on the floor, leaning against the bed and rubbing her bare feet against the soft plush of Miranda's rug. The best part of going to a formal was always the hour before getting ready and the hour afterward rehashing the night—so who cared if they'd pretty much skipped the middle? "And how about the way Peter King kept drooling every time I walked by?"

"Peter the Perv? Didn't he get thrown out of school last year for trying to install that camera in the girls' locker room?" Miranda asked with a laugh, almost choking on a kernel of popcorn.

"He's b-a-a-a-a-ack," Harper sang out.

"Hey, at least you didn't have Lawrence Lester and the bug thugs chasing after you all night," Miranda complained.

"Lester Lawrence," Harper corrected her sternly. "Lester and Miranda Lawrence—has a nice ring to it, don't you think?"

"Shut up!" Miranda slammed a pillow into Harper's face and they both dissolved into giggles. There were a lot of kids in their high school, and most of them sucked—if they tried hard enough, this could keep them going all night long.

chapter

17

"Dude, great party!" Adam said, stumbling through the doorway of the motel. Beth caught him just before he fell.

"Yeah, great," she echoed weakly, taking in the cloud of smoke, stench of beer, pumping music, and scattered couples making out in the darkened corners.

Adam high-fived Kane. "Your brother manage to score us the kegs?"

"You know it," Kane assured him.

"Awesome—point me to it, liquor-man."

"Adam," Beth began tentatively, "don't you think maybe you've had enough?"

He brushed her off and charged ahead. "No such thing!" he called back, before disappearing into the darkness.

Beth froze in the lobby, not sure what to do. A few tinted paper lanterns hung from the ceiling, casting an eerie, shadowy pall over everything. There was no electricity, and they'd decided against candles (nice ambience but overwhelming likelihood of disaster), so they were stuck with the dim reddish lighting of the battery-powered lanterns and the few shafts of moonlight filtering in through the lobby windows.

She and Adam had been one of the last couples to leave the dance, so all the seniors on the secret invite list had already showed up—the place was packed, but in the darkness, Beth couldn't pick out any familiar faces. There were only strangers, blank bodies bouncing in time with the music or squeezed in together on one of the couches, ignoring the crowd. She was so tired, and so alone.

And she'd been feeling that way for hours—despite glimpses of sobriety and sweet moments of romance, Adam had spent the end of the night in a vodka haze, laughing it up with his friends while Beth stood awkwardly on the fringes, with only Kaia to talk to. And so, with no one to talk to at all.

Now she was on the fringes again, with Adam nowhere to be seen. She felt invisible, and yet totally exposed. As if everyone in the room was watching her, knowing with certainty that she didn't belong. And indeed, if it weren't for the Adam connection, she never would have been there—all of her old friends were probably home in bed, or sitting up in Lara Tanner's basement eating ice cream and watching old black-and-white movies. Much as she wished she was with them, she just didn't belong there anymore—too bad she didn't seem to belong here, either.

She looked around in vain for someone she knew, someone she could talk to—even Kaia, at this point, would have been a relief. But it was as if the moment they'd stepped through the door together, everyone else had been pulled off into some kind of vortex. Vanished. And here she was, alone.

She supposed this wasn't the kind of party where you made small talk, anyway. It was the kind where you passed out on one of the dusty couches, or threw yourself into a sweaty mass of dancers—or you did what she'd come here to do.

She could always go home, she guessed. Call a taxi, get out of here, escape. Forget this night had ever happened, forget about the supposed fresh start, about what she'd been planning to do. Save it for some other time.

The place was a skanky mess.

Adam had morphed into a drunken idiot.

But Beth had waited long enough to know that perfection wasn't coming—tonight was just going to have to do.

And maybe finding the keg first wasn't such a bad idea.

"Think we can go somewhere a bit more ... private?" Kaia whispered to Kane, running a hand down the small of his back.

"Say no more."

They threaded their way through the crowd in the lobby, away from the flickering light and the echoing music. Up the stairs, down a long, dark, narrow hallway, ignoring the shadowy shapes pressed against the walls, the bodies writhing together. Into a small, dark room at the end of the hall, the faded drapes drawn, allowing a slash of moonlight to cut through the room. It lit Kaia's hands as she slowly unbuttoned Kane's shirt. Their bodies remained in shadow, figures silhouetted against the night.

"Not quite the penthouse suite," Kane admitted ruefully, his fingers expertly unhooking her bra as they stumbled together toward the bed.

"Not quite." Kaia lay back and pulled him down on top of her, pressing herself against his tight body, relishing the heavy weight bearing down on her. "But it'll do." And so would Kane. He wasn't the catch he imagined himself to be—but he was hot, he was cocky, and, most importantly, he was there. Sometimes Kaia needed a challenge—but sometimes she just needed a break.

She pulled him toward her, closed her eyes, and let herself go.

Along with copious amounts of alcohol, Kane had also supplied the party with two wooden barrels filled with condoms, positioned considerately just inside the door.

As Adam blundered off in search of more to drink, Beth had surreptitiously grabbed one and slipped it into her purse—and then, on second thought, she'd grabbed a handful more.

Now, an hour further into the night, her bold act was beginning to seem like a total waste. They were still down in the lobby amidst a group of Adam's drunken teammates; Beth's head was throbbing, and as Adam regaled a cluster of admirers with a story of last year's basketball triumph, he leaned against her heavily, as if without her support he would drop to the ground.

"Adam, let's take off," she whispered urgently, when he finally stopped talking.

"You wanna go home?" he slurred. "Party's just starting. Right, guys?"

The "guys," whose shunted-aside dates all looked

about as nonplussed as Beth felt, let out a hearty cheer of support.

"Not home," she explained in a low voice. *"Upstairs."*

"She wants to go upstairs!" he crowed to the crowd. "Lez go, honey. You want me, you got me."

Irritated and humiliated—but knowing how hard it had been to prepare herself for this night and determined to finally go through with it—Beth allowed Adam to shepherd her into the dark bowels of the hotel, where they finally found an unoccupied room and slipped inside.

"Beth," he said, seeming to sober up a bit now that he was away from the noise and the people and the stench of beer, "I feel like shit. Maybe we should just head home."

"I don't think you want to go home yet, Adam. This is your lucky day," she said, trying to sound more brazen than she felt. Beth had never had to make a first move in her life, and she had no idea what to do. But how hard could it be? All guys ever wanted was sex, any time, all the time, right? So she just needed to let him know that a new option had been added to the menu, and hopefully he'd do the rest.

"I want you, Adam," she said in what she hoped was a sexy voice. "Now."

She pushed him down on the bed, and he landed with a thud, knocking his head against the wooden headboard.

Oops.

"Jesus, are you trying to kill me?" he shouted, rubbing the back of his head.

"I'm sorry, I'm sorry." She hopped into the bed, kissing the bruise gently. "This isn't going the way I wanted it to."

"What isn't?" he asked in confusion.

"This. Tonight. Right now," she told him, kissing him again, more urgently.

"What's right now?"

Why couldn't he just *get* it? Why was he making this so hard for her?

"Right now is when—when I tell you that I'm finally ready," Beth admitted. She bit the inside of her cheek and nervously waited for him to say something. Who knows—maybe he didn't even want her anymore. Maybe that's what all this had been about.

He sat up, couldn't see her face in the darkness, but reached out a hand to touch her cheek, as if trying to read her expression.

"Ready? For . . . ?"

She nodded, and then realized he couldn't see her. "Yes."

"Now?"

"Yes." And she kissed him, and he kissed her back, eagerly, hungrily, and they rolled over on the bed together, drinking each other in, their bodies lost in each other, and then—they stopped.

Beth tensed, her back clenched and her muscles stiffening, as they always did, just before she reached the point of no return. He pulled away, and she lay on her back, breathing quickly, glad it was too dark for him to see the tears that were leaking from her tightly closed eyes.

"Beth?" came his warm voice in the darkness. "Beth, are you sure you're ready for this?"

No.

No.

"Yes."

She groped for her purse on the night table, pulled out one of the condoms, and tossed it to him.

"I mean, we're in love, right?" she asked. "I love you, you love me, we're adults. This is the right thing to do." It came out sounding like a question.

There was a long pause, and then, "Yeah, we're in love," he agreed. And he sounded almost sure.

"I just—I just need a minute," she promised him. "Then I'll be ready."

He reached over and found her hand, and she clenched it tightly, and they lay side by side on the musty bed. She stared up at the cracked ceiling and breathed deeply, in and out, picturing his body lying next to hers, so close, and how it would be to have him inside of her, to be with him, to lose herself in him. To finally let herself go.

She tried to unclench her muscles, reminded herself that she loved him, she wanted him—and she did, so much that it terrified her. For if she let that wave of emotion, of pleasure, sweep her away, how would she ever find her way back?

Breathe in.

Breathe out.

She had to do this, and she had to do it now—because one thing she knew, one thing was certain: She didn't want to lose him.

"I'm ready," she whispered to herself. "Adam? I'm ready," she said louder.

There was no response, and his hand was still.

"Adam?"

She rolled over on her side, kissed his cheek, his lips, then propped herself up, her face suspended a few inches from his. His still, peaceful face. Eyes closed. Breath slow and even.

And then—a snore.

Beth flopped down again on her back, next to him.

Unbelievable.

She had been dressed like a fairy-tale princess—and was trapped in the wrong story. In her story, Prince Charming decorated the room with a thousand candles, took her in his arms, and sweetly, gently, took her away with him. In her story, a handsome boy and a beautiful girl danced the night away at the ball and swept off into the sunset. They swore their everlasting love to each other. They lived happily ever after.

Not this story. Not this night.

In this story, the wrong story, she lay atop a grungy bedspread, a hard and creaky mattress, in a slimy motel room, groping in the darkness and ignoring the moans and thuds seeping through the paper-thin walls.

In this story, Prince Charming was a drunken clod who passed out and left her alone.

Beth lay very still, listening to his even breathing and trying to forget the night, though it hadn't yet ended. The hours stretched ahead of her, a desert of time. So much for her perfect night; so much for her fairy tale.

This is not the way it was supposed to be, Beth thought, closing her eyes and wishing for sleep. *This is not the way it was supposed to be.*

This is not the way it was supposed to be, Harper thought, scuffing her weary feet against the pavement. She'd left Miranda's house elated, the alcohol and pot and laughter fusing into the perfect painkiller.

But over the long walk home, strappy heels in hand, her mood had changed.

When she reached her house, she took a few steps up the stone walkway to the front door, then stopped. Her parents, as always, thought she was sleeping at Miranda's, so it's not like they were waiting up. There was no reason to go inside—not yet. She veered around the house and found her way into the backyard. She clambered up to the flat top of her rock—their rock—and shivered in the chilly night breeze.

Somehow, everything had gone wrong.

It was her senior year. It was the night of the party. Her party. She wasn't supposed to spend the night rolling joints with Miranda—she was supposed to be with Adam, happy, in love. Not bitter, not alone.

It was only a few weeks into the school year, and everything, *everything* was wrong.

And there was no way in hell that she was going to take it anymore.

She was Harper Grace. Alone and pathetic, jealous and bitter were not her style. *Tears* were not her style, she reminded herself. She angrily wiped them away, then sat up and pulled out her cell phone. Typed in a familiar number, then began composing her text message.

She hesitated for a moment, hand hovering over the keys, thinking about the night she'd just spent with Miranda, the loyal friend who stayed with her through everything, who always rescued her, who always got her through.

She thought about a promise she'd made, a promise that she'd meant.

And then she thought about Adam—about Adam and Kaia, the embrace she still saw every time she closed her eyes. About Adam and Beth, who were probably together right now, hand in hand, body on body, flesh against flesh.

There are some things more important than friendship, Harper decided. Some things more important than promises.

And, hoping she was right, she hit send.

Kane was likely busy right now, she knew, but sometime tomorrow he'd wake up, slough off his hangover, and read her message: If offer is still open—I'm in.

Here's a taste of the next *sinful* read . . .

Envy

They'd needed somewhere out of the way, somewhere no one they knew would ever be or would ever think to look for them. The school library was an obvious choice. Huddled over a small table in the back (sandwiched in the stacks between self-help and pet grooming), Harper and Kane quickly got down to business.

"It's a good start, Grace, but we need to kick it into higher gear. Slow and steady's not going to win us the race on this one," Kane whispered.

Harper craned her neck around, once again making sure that no one she knew could overhear them. Her crowd wasn't much for the musty book zone, it was true—but a certain brainy Barbie clone had been known to stop by.

"I don't know, Kane—that relationship has a definite expiration date. And with Beth fawning all over you for the next two weeks, maybe . . ."

"Adam will have enough space to discover you're the best thing ever to happen to him?" Kane finished for her.

Harper blushed. That was, in fact, exactly what she'd been thinking. "Well, if you want to put it that way."

"Wake up, Harper," Kane said sharply, snapping his fingers in front of her face. "These two could go on like this indefinitely. They're both too noble to cut their losses. I know Adam, and he's going to stay in this to the bitter end, and Beth—"

"Couldn't stand on her own two feet if you nailed them to the floor and shoved a pole up her—"

"Hey, watch how you talk about my woman."

"*Your* woman?" She arched an impeccably plucked eyebrow. "Someone's getting a little ahead of himself."

"Exactly my point—I don't like waiting, and I didn't think you did either. Isn't that why we're in this thing?"

"Okay," she conceded. "So we've got the setup, Adam's already jealous—"

"And soon it will start to fester—," Kane added.

"Especially if we help it along a bit." Harper concluded. *So* not a problem. If there was one thing she could handle, it was feeding the flames of jealousy—hadn't she proved that well enough over the weekend? "But we need something else, something more dramatic, with a little flair."

"I couldn't agree more. But what?" Kane asked. They were right back to where they'd started. "That's the million-dollar question. And it has to be done right, with finesse—we don't want this to backfire."

"Are you thinking of something specific?"

"I'm just trying to ensure that we *both* get what we want," Kane explained, winking, "since, never let it be said I think only of myself . . ."

Harper raised both eyebrows this time.

"Okay, usually I do," he admitted. "But in this case, we're in it together—one for all, all for one, et cetera."

"Whatever, I'll believe it when I see it. I've known you for too long."

"Oh, you wound me!" he exclaimed. Mrs. Martin, the ancient and evil-eyed librarian, walked by and gave them a nasty look. The shut-up-or-get-out kind of look. Harper lowered her eyes and tried to muster a chaste and innocent smile. But Mrs. Martin, immune to the act, just scuttled on by.

"I'm supposed to trust you?" Harper asked, lowering her voice to a whisper. "When you're trying to steal your best friend's girlfriend?"

All traces of a smirk vanished from Kane's face, and he glared at her with hooded eyes.

"First of all, Grace, I don't believe in trust—which is why I don't believe in best friends. It's easier that way. And second of all, as for stealing his girlfriend . . ."

Harper leaned forward eagerly. She'd been wondering how Kane could justify his scheming, especially when he seemed to have no particular motivation for choosing Beth, of all the girls he could have pursued.

". . . let's just say—karma's a bitch."

"Care to elaborate?" Harper asked.

"No."

They stared at each other in silence for a moment, each daring the other to speak. Harper broke first.

"Fine—just get back to what you were saying," Harper urged him. "What kind of backfiring are you afraid of?"

"Well, we could pin something on Adam, like, say, he

slept with someone else—believable enough, I guess," Kane said, his smirk returning. "Deep down, all guys are pigs."

Harper opened her mouth—then closed it again. She couldn't betray Adam's confidence. At least not until she heard all of what Kane had to say.

"That could work," she mused.

He shook his head slowly but surely. "Not so much—think about it. Beth breaks up with Adam in a fit of anger, and Adam spends the rest of his life trying to win her back. And I don't think either of us wants to deal with that."

"Agreed," Harper said, her heart sinking. He was right—and she had nothing. Nothing that wouldn't turn Harper and Adam's potential relationship into collateral damage. "In fact, I think Adam needs to be the one to break it off," she concluded in spite of herself. "He feels betrayed, she feels unjustly wronged, they both want nothing to do with each other and go running into our arms."

"Sounds like the perfect plan. Except . . ." Kane sighed in exasperation. "We still need to figure out how to get from point A to point B."

"We'll figure it out," she comforted him. "In the meantime we continue to drive Adam out of his mind with jealousy?"

"You got it. And, hey, never underestimate the power of the Kane Geary charisma. For all I know, a couple more of these study 'dates' and she'll be begging *me* to hit the bedroom."

Harper balled up a piece of paper and tossed it at his big, fat head. "Leaving Adam ready and waiting for some sympathetic TLC from his beautiful next door neighbor?" she suggested sarcastically. "Unlikely."

"Hey, you never know—it could happen."

It's not like Miranda had no one to eat lunch with. No, she reassured herself, she had plenty of friends. Just because Harper had randomly decided to skip out on lunch didn't mean Miranda was adrift on some sea of loserdom. There were plenty of people she *could* sit with, plenty who would covet her presence at their table if only because the reflected beams of Harper's glory made Miranda glow with the light of borrowed popularity. But the prospect of pushing "food" around on her tray while listening to the stupid simpering of these so-called friends—without Harper across the table to exchange timely eye rolls with—was just too much for her to handle this afternoon. So instead, Miranda opted for a snack machine lunch (granola bar and mini canister of Pringles) at the newspaper office, which had a door that locked and a couch that creaked noisily but had yet to collapse.

But first, a pit stop at the girls' bathroom. She stood in front of the mirror, touching up her makeup—and making a mental note that a makeup makeover would definitely have to be her next stop on the road to self-improvement. The peach frosted lip gloss and smoky gray eye shadow she'd picked out in tenth grade just wouldn't do. Her mother, though usually having more than enough to say on the subject of Miranda's appearance—and how to improve it—knew nothing about makeup herself. She'd been able to contribute very little to Miranda's education on the subject beyond such helpful pointers as "That blush makes you look like a whore."

The bathroom was surprisingly uncrowded for this time of day. A couple stoners lurked in the back corner, from the sound of it competing over who had more Phish bootlegs. A cluster of super-skinny bottle blondes—Miranda didn't recognize them, so figured they must be freshmen—hogged most of the mirror area, reapplying their hairspray and shimmery lipstick. From the short skirts to the perfect manicures to the cocky tilt of their heads Miranda could tell they were jockeying for a place in the line of succession, ready to fill the power vacuum once Harper had graduated. *Cosmo* clones, Miranda thought disdainfully. They could look the part all they wanted, but they'd never have that spark, that something special Harper had that made people want to follow her to the ends of the earth (or at least to the end of good judgment). Harper was a leader. These girls—it was obvious—were sheep.

And yet . . .

And yet, she thought, looking from one perfectly sculpted and outfitted body to the next, wasn't this exactly the look she was craving?

Long, silky smooth hair that could bounce and blow in the wind—Miranda's hair was brittle, thin, and impossibly flat. Flawless complexions—Miranda had zits and freckles. Long, slim, tanned legs—Miranda's thunder thighs were albino pale.

The girls bustled out of the bathroom, chattering about who had hooked up that weekend and who was feeling fat. Big surprise—unanimous responses to both.

Miranda sighed and considered trying to score some pot off the stoners in the corner, anything to calm the rising tide of anxiety she suddenly felt at the daunting prospect of finding a way to turn herself into *that*. Not that she wanted to be vapid, of course. But beautiful? Stylish? *Skinny?* The kind of girl who screams "high maintenance" but which, it seemed, was all any worthwhile guy wanted?

Yes, please.

Haven High was a small school. Claustrophobically small, it sometimes seemed to Adam. But he'd done a decent job so far of avoiding Kaia. He hadn't spoken to her, in fact, since their last encounter. He still shuddered at the thought of it—the intense, mind-blowing sex in an abandoned motel, followed almost immediately by an utterly humiliating blow-off. What a loser he'd been. He saw that now. It was too late, of course—he'd done it, this huge, horrible thing that weighed on him, crushed him, and yet still flickered through his fantasies, taunting him with what he couldn't have yet still, in some deep part of him, wanted.

Beth had wondered why he suddenly stopped following Kaia around and inviting her out with the group, but she had no fond feelings for Kaia herself, so hadn't wondered very long or very loudly. And maybe she didn't want to know.

Still, it was a small school, and he'd been bound to bump into Kaia eventually. He just hadn't counted on a literal collision.

"Oh, sorry!" he exclaimed, after spinning away from his locker and slamming into someone rushing past him down the hall. Then—"Oh, it's you." Suddenly, the split-second collision became, in his mind, an embrace, as if he could still feel the ghostly touch of his body pressing against hers, their hands and chests and hips awkwardly rubbing against each other, her silky hair whipping across his face.

"And it's you, too," she pointed out. "Where've you been, stranger?"

"Far away from you, which I thought was how you wanted it." Her words to him at their last meeting echoed through his head. And the mocking laughter.

"Oh, Adam, I hope I didn't hurt your feelings." She placed a soft hand on his chest—he pushed it away. "I don't know what I'd do if I thought you hated me!"

"Give it up, Kaia," he said harshly. "I'm not falling for your crap again. Find someone new to screw over."

Kaia rolled her eyes. "Oh, right," she scoffed. "You're such the wounded victim, used and abused, right? You didn't seem to mind the screwing part so much."

"Shut up," he hissed, suddenly aware of the students swarming around them. Watching. Listening? "I thought we agreed you weren't going to tell anyone about that."

"Oh, calm down. My lips are sealed. Why would I do anything to get between you and your precious Beth?"

"I appreciate that, Kaia." He tried to ignore the disdainful edge to her voice. Kaia, he'd decided, was like a venomous snake—you just had to be very careful, stay very still, and wait her out until she got bored and went away.

"Of course," she added, smirking, "maybe I'm not the one you need to worry about."

"What's that supposed to mean?" he asked, against his better judgment.

"I saw your blushing rose getting cozy in the coffee shop with your supposed best friend the other day. Just thought you'd want to know."

"Old news," he said, affecting nonchalance. Ignoring the taste of bile. "She's tutoring him for the SATs. I know all about it. And it's completely innocent." And this he believed wholeheartedly, he told himself. He had to, right?

"So I heard. Such a sweet girl, to commit her time to helping him, when she's oh so busy. But totally innocent, of course," she assured him, voice dripping with false sincerity. "I'm sure you're right. Just another platonic extracurricular, like any other: yearbook, newspaper, party planning . . ."

She narrowed her gaze suggestively and Adam felt the tips of his ears turn red. It was, after all, planning a party that had brought Adam and Kaia together in the first place. A few week's worth of purely platonic meetings culminating in one night of illicit but extraordinary passion.

"I'm sure you have nothing to worry about, though," she said after a moment of silence. "I mean, you're in love, right? And that's what love is all about—trust."

Trust. Right.

If Beth's love for him proved as trustworthy as his love for her, they were in for some serious problems.

Job well done, Kaia congratulated herself. Adam had, of course, walked away from her in disgust, but she could see the beginnings of doubt in the nervous twist of his lip and the tiny rivulets of sweat that traced a path down the muscles of his neck. She'd gotten under his skin—again.

Kaia laughed to herself. It probably wasn't very nice of her to pick on Adam again. After all, he was such an easy mark, and clearly still smarting from their last encounter.

On the other hand, she considered, she'd given him a true gift—one that he'd certainly enjoyed enough at the time, no matter how much he may now claim she'd ruined his life. Didn't she deserve to have some fun too? And if it was fun at Beth Manning's expense, even better. Much as she tried, she couldn't forget the fact that Mr. Powell had chosen that simpering softie over her. Yes, it was clearly because he thought Kaia spelled trouble, while Beth would be easy prey. Powell was a predator; it was why she liked him so much. But still, there it was—he'd rejected her in favor of Beth, and while that was a lapse in judgment she was willing to forgive, Beth still needed to pay.

This time, she'd decided, there was no reason to go it alone. Not when such a good game was already afoot.

So she headed to the library. She'd spotted Harper heading in that direction at the beginning of lunch period, and she had a sneaking suspicion she'd find her huddled over a desk with Kane, hatching some pathetic plan. It was time to lend these small-town tricksters the wisdom of her experience.

Why?

Why the hell not?

She found them just as she'd imagined, heads together, arms waving animatedly, whispers flying. She crept up slowly behind Harper, finger to her lips, trusting Kane to keep his poker face, which he did, right up to the moment that Kaia tapped Harper on the shoulder and smiled angelically into her face, which reflected, in quick succession, surprise, guilt, and disgust. Harper settled on the latter, but Kaia kept up her icy smile.

"What do you want?" Harper hissed. "We're busy here."

"I don't mind if the lovely Kaia joins us," Kane said generously.

"Shut up, Kane." Harper glared at him, then turned back to Kaia. "Why are you still here?"

"What, is this where you tell me, 'This is an *A, B* conversation, and I should *C* my way out of it?'" Kaia sneered.

"I was leaning more toward, 'This is an *X, Z* conversation, so *Y* don't you just go away,'" Harper corrected her. "Or at least I *would* have been if this were 1998 and we were ten years old. What do you think this is, VH1's *Lamest Slang of the '90s*?"

"Well, your outfit does say 'retro gone wrong,'" Kaia pointed out. "but I guess you're not out of time, just out of taste. I can live with that."

"I'm supposed to take fashion tips from someone who makes Paris Hilton look classy?" Harper scoffed.

Kane, whose eyes had been bouncing back and forth between the two as if he were following a heated Ping-Pong match, began to softly applaud. "Bring it on, ladies. When do we take out the mud wrestling pit?"

"Shut up, Kane," they snapped in unison.

He chuckled softly. "Okay, okay, I know when I'm not wanted." He checked his watch and stood up, collecting his books. "Besides," he gave Harper a meaningful look, "I've got to go meet someone. We're setting up a study 'date' for later. See ya."

Harper shot him a vicious, how-dare-you-leave-me-here-alone-with-*her* look, but he just grinned and disappeared.

"Such a studious guy all of a sudden," Kaia commented.

"Yeah, well, you know Kane, needs to win at all costs," Harper said uncomfortably. "Even if it means some hard work."

"It's going to be pretty damn hard to win at the rate you two are going," Kaia pointed out.

"What's that supposed to mean?"

Kaia laughed to herself. It would have been cute if it weren't so pathetic, this little show of ignorance and innocence. Harper was going to have to work on the poker face a bit if this whole thing was going to work.

"I think you know," Kaia said simply.

Harper sighed. "Kaia, it's a little early in the week for mind games, don't you think?"

"Look I didn't come here to fight, or play games," Kaia promised her, wishing they could just cut through the bullshit and skip to the part where they got something done. But, as she well knew, that's not how these things worked. And the bullshit was, in the end, half the fun. "At least, not with you."

"Then what?" Harper asked wearily.

"I know what you're up to," Kaia said, relishing the involuntary shudder that ran through Harper's body. "And I want to help."

"You know what we're up to? Are you talking in code now? What is this, a James Bond movie? What would we be 'up to'?"

"Do you really want me to spell it out for you? Adam, Beth, Operation Screw Over Your Supposed Best Friend—or, in your case, just screw him?"

Harper's face turned pale. "I don't know what you're talking about," she claimed in a strangled voice.

"Yeah, yeah, whatever you say. You're totally innocent, you're appalled I would even suggest it. Whatever." Kaia checked her watch. This was getting old. "Here's my point. I want to help—you two are playing out of your league, and I think you need some coaching from a pro. That's me."

"Just out of curiosity," and it was clear that Harper had plenty, "let's say Kane and I did have some unholy alliance—why would *you* want to help? And why would we trust you?"

"I'm helping because I'm bored, and because I hate to see a good opportunity go to waste. As for why you should trust me?" Kaia paused. It was a good question. One that deserved a reasonably honest answer. "You shouldn't. But you're going to anyway because you've got almost everything you need—will, motive, lack of scruples—but you're missing one key thing, and that's what I can supply."

"And what's that?" Harper asked skeptically.

"A plan."

about the author

Robin Wasserman enjoys writing about high school—but wakes up every day grateful that she doesn't have to relive it. She recently abandoned the beaches and boulevards of Los Angeles for the chilly embrace of the East Coast, as all that sun and fun gave her too little to complain about. She now lives and writes in New York City, which she claims to love for its vibrant culture and intellectual life. In reality, she doesn't make it to museums nearly enough, and actually just loves the city for its pizza, its shopping, and the fact that at three a.m. you can always get anything you need—and you can get it delivered.

As many as 1 in 3 Americans
who have HIV... don't know it.

TAKE CONTROL.
KNOW YOUR STATUS.
GET TESTED.

To learn more about HIV testing,
or get a free guide to HIV and
other sexually transmitted diseases:

www.knowhivaids.org
1-866-344-KNOW

FEARLESS FBI

Special Agent, Gaia Moore

Francine Pascal's bestselling Fearless series is all grown-up. Gaia's out of college and training for the FBI. Solving real cases, tracking real criminals . . . it takes strength, intelligence, and fierce determination.

But while the FBI has strict codes and procedures, Gaia has never been a team player.

And when it comes to hunting down a serial killer, cracking the case may mean bending FBI rules. For Gaia, it means breaking them.

#1 KILL GAME

#2 LIVE BAIT

By Francine Pascal

From Simon Pulse • Published by Simon & Schuster

Sharper. Older. More dangerous than ever.

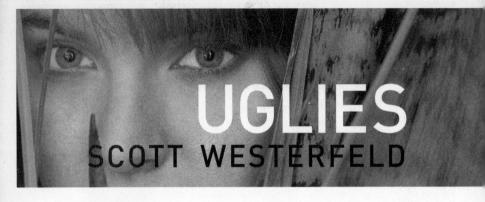

UGLIES
SCOTT WESTERFELD

Everybody gets to be supermodel gorgeous. What could be wrong with that?

In this futuristic world, all children are born "uglies," or freaks. But on their sixteenth birthdays they are given extreme makeovers and turned "pretty." Then their whole lives change. . . .

PRAISE FOR *UGLIES*:

★ "An exciting series. . . . The awesome ending thrills with potential."
— *Kirkus Reviews*

★ "Ingenious . . . high-concept YA fiction that has wide appeal."
— *Booklist*

★ "Highly readable with a convincing plot that incorporates futuristic technologies and a disturbing commentary on our current public policies. Fortunately, the cliff-hanger ending promises a sequel."
— *School Library Journal*

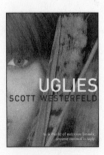

And
coming soon:
SPECIALS

PUBLISHED BY SIMON PULSE